THE NEEDLE ENDS

A NOVEL

MAREN CLIFF

Copyright © 2025 by Maren Cliff

25 26 27 28 29   5 4 3 2 1

Please send all permission queries to the publisher:

Maren Cliff Publishing

marencliffauthor@gmail.com

Maren Cliff c/o Bishop Koch Lawyers

10 – 3092 Dunmore Road SE

Medicine Hat, AB T1B 2X2

This novel is a work of fiction. Although some long-standing and public offices are mentioned, they are used fictitiously, and all characters, events, incidents, and dialogue are the products of the author's imagination. Any resemblance to actual persons, living or dead, or actual events is purely coincidental.

Cataloguing data available from Library and Archives Canada

ISBN (pbk): 978-1-7387738-2-4

ISBN (epub): 978-1-7387738-3-1

Cover Design and Layout: Laura Boyle

Developmental Editing: Sarah Harvey

Copyediting: Dawn Loewen

Proofreading: Fern Derie

"I am writing this book because
we're all going to die"

-Jack Kerouac

CONTENT WARNING

This story includes
episodes of violence and
references to suicide.

PROLOGUE

The IV was already running when the doctor arrived. The patient, an elderly man, was sitting in his favorite burgundy leather chair, facing a large picture window that displayed the splendor of a manicured and extensively landscaped backyard. Sitting next to the man, on a folding chair, was his wife. She had a wad of tissue in her hand and had obviously been crying, but was now forcing a smile and a laugh. The focus of her attention was split between her fragile husband and a small, hyper dog, currently wrestling the slipper on her husband's foot as he weakly but good-naturedly teased it with the tassels.

The house was somehow abuzz and preternaturally still at the same time. The doctor counted twenty-two people present, ranging in age from young teens to a man at least a few years older than the patient himself. Four slow cookers were burbling in the kitchen, and the smell of homemade soup and fresh buns was intoxicating to the doctor, who had yet to stop for a bite to eat that day.

The doctor had come straight from the hospital pharmacy, where he had collected the medication, packaged in a horribly conspicuous but highly functional compartmentalized gray plastic suitcase. The meds were reviewed with the attending pharmacist in a choreographed dance of bureaucratic box-ticking. The doctor always marveled at how much extra effort was put into the regulation of the medications in this circumstance, when their only function was to end the life of the patient who had requested them. The doctor had seen, and probably himself performed, a kind of five-second rule: a vial of meds dropped on the floor, quickly wiped with alcohol, and then administered to a patient who was fully expected to live a long and healthy life afterward. The drugs he was administering today were prepared in a sterile fume hood, despite the fact their intended recipient would not, in any universe, survive long enough to develop any type of infection. The doctor's actions were carefully observed and scrutinized at all steps, even though the intended outcome here was the one conclusion against which most doctors fought all their battles.

The doctor laid the bulky suitcase of drugs down behind the chair and crouched to reintroduce himself to the patient and his wife, having previously met them for a long discussion about three weeks prior. The assisting nurse had attended even more "provisions," as these events were called, than the doctor, fast becoming the expert and steady guiding hand for most medical assistance in dying—MAID—in their small city. She was a retired ICU nurse and, even several years after leaving the hospital environment, the doctor was pretty sure she could start an IV in a stone—a feat no more difficult than starting a line in a frail hand ravaged by disease, by chemo, and eventually by resignation to the impending oblivion. The doctor placed his hand on his patient's arm and it was immediately enveloped by both the patient's hand and his wife's, forming an unspoken pact: as a team, today they would help him find peace.

The nurse then gently directed everyone, including the patient's wife, into the other room so that the doctor could get the final consent from his patient. The discussion was brief. Capacity to consent did not require a patient to recite the alphabet backward or to remember the name of their first-grade teacher. What the doctor needed to confirm was that the patient knew why the doctor was there and whether or not the patient wanted to proceed to end his life today. The answer was clear and affirmatory, which it most often, although not always, was at this point in the long and highly regulated assisted dying process. The final paperwork was completed and the doctor stepped briefly into the other room to prepare the family. The doctor described the process and the chance that they might see or hear symptoms such as snoring respirations or cyanosis of the lips. He also reassured them the process would be peaceful and quick and that he was there to ensure their cherished one was cared for and surrounded by love and support until his last breath. He invited any further questions, then advised the family they were welcome to go back to the patient now, to say their goodbyes; they could let him and the nurse know when they were ready. The doctor reassured the family there was no rush; he and his colleague were here only for them. As the doctor and the nurse waited in the kitchen discussing recent legislation changes and reviewing paperwork quietly among themselves, they could hear crying, laughing, and music in the other room. One of the teenagers had been requested by the patient to play the piano, and she was playing a shaky but lovely compilation of Chopin nocturnes prepared for an upcoming examination.

A short while later, the patient's eldest son put in motion the final moments with a simple "He's ready." Several family members elected to wait on the deck rather than be present, their fear of the unknown much worse than anything that was about to occur. Several others sat on the floor in front of their loved one, and a daughter-in-law pulled up another chair to support the wife. The piano solo continued.

The doctor once again touched his patient's arm, then whispered gently, "I'm going to take good care of you, are you ready?" The patient nodded. Soon the first medicine began its short journey to the heart of the matter, inducing a pleasant euphoria, an effect that would gladly have been shared by all those present, the medical staff included. The patient's eyes got heavy in only a few minutes as the second medication chased the other to offer its particular attributes. After a short dose of lidocaine to numb the vein, a likely superfluous step given the patient's already pharmacologically induced rest, the propofol followed in short order. The doctor would never say so at this stage, but given propofol's unique creamy white color, it had many nicknames. When the doctor had been training at the children's hospital, it was called "Polar Bear Milk," a simplistic attempt to friendly-up the medications coursing into tiny and frightened young veins. In the OR, it was called "Vitamin P," because no one could ever have enough propofol; it was jokingly referred to as "good for what ails you." In this context, the doctor always thought of it as the "Milk of Human Kindness" because he really believed his being there, taking on this work, was a kindness he could provide to patients who had not recently experienced much kindness from Fate herself.

The propofol had very quickly done its job; the patient was unconscious, snoring gently until that bodily function stopped slowly. The doctor had kept an eye on pulsations in the patient's neck and at this stage they still continued, although the family was now sobbing, knowing their loved one was leaving them. The faint undulations of the neck stopped soon after, well before the final medication, a paralytic, was administered to seal the deal. The doctor stood behind the patient as the family came forward to kiss him, to say goodbye, and to let their tears fall upon him one last time. When all the medications had been administered, the doctor used a stethoscope to listen to the patient's chest. The chest does not sound silent after death—it is more a hollow echo that feels as though it is trying to trick the listener into hearing life where there is none. But having been a physician for many years, the doctor was not to be fooled. He announced gently but clearly to the family that the patient was gone and announced to the nurse the time of death. He placed his hand on the wife's shoulder and said how sorry he was for their loss and how grateful he was that he had met the patient and was able to help him. He stated with total sincerity that it was clear the patient was a special man who was well loved not only in death, but in life as well, and that he wished that everyone could be surrounded by such love in their final moments.

Several of the family members came to shake the doctor's hand, and the nurse handed out more tissue and gave the patient's wife an intense and meaningful embrace. The nurse spoke to the eldest son to confirm the funeral home chosen and asked if they wanted her to remain with them until the funeral home arrived. They didn't feel that was necessary, so she instead reiterated the next steps and also ensured they had her contact information for any questions that might arise. The doctor disconnected the infusion line from the patient's IV and they packed up their supplies and paperwork to take back to the hospital to complete while returning the unused medications. The family placed a blanket over the patient but only over his lap and chest, not his head, and he remained in his favorite chair surrounded by his loved ones. The dog hopped up on his lap and settled in as the doctor closed the front door behind him.

At the hospital, the medications were returned and signed over, the medical examiner was advised of the death, and the paperwork was double-checked and signed by all involved. The doctor and nurse had little to debrief, the provision having gone as smoothly as they had come to expect. Most of their patients had already lost control of bodily functions, all had surrendered future plans and goals for life, and before choosing MAID many had even lost control of the freight train that is medical intervention. A runaway tram on a unidirectional track, chugging along toward a curative destination that was not even located on that line. Medical care had become a fancy and technological locomotive that was not only solely purposed, but also too often lacking any braking system. The doctor didn't see himself as the brakeman, as some patients wanted to persevere with treatment and that was their choice. He saw himself, and the option of a medically assisted death, as a railway switch, allowing the train to exit, to slow, and to reach the same ultimate destination, but on a track of beauty, reflection, and choice, rather than careening toward the same inevitable crash. The doctor was reflecting on the life of his patient, and on his place in both the life and death of so many of his patients, as he exited the pharmacy. He then headed directly to the ward down the hall to finish his general rounds for the day; it was his job to carry on.

CHAPTER 1

The bottle tumbled to the ground and glass shattered, liquid spreading everywhere on the partially completed floor. Rivien swore under her breath while thanking the grape gods that it was a bottle of white instead of a red that would have stained the floor like a crime scene. As she went to retrieve the dust pan and mop she smiled to herself, the realization never growing old that one should not cry over spilled wine.

"What was that?" Rivien's mother, Marcia, called from the back room.

"Just broke a bottle."

"Mama, you crazy" came a tiny voice, accompanied by tiny pounding footsteps growing closer.

"Rita, NO!" shouted Marcia, as Rivien whipped around in time to roughly grab her child away from the shattered glass.

"Ow...Mama, you hurt me." Tears came quickly, distrust filling Rita's wide eyes.

"Nugget...I'm sorry," Rivien said. "But I can't let you get cut in the glass, you have to be careful."

"But you hurt me."

"I'm sorry, honey, I didn't mean to. Jeez, Mom, couldn't you stop her?" Rivien said, angry that her child felt hurt, angrier still that she was blamed.

"I'm sorry, but I'm not really sure what you think I can do? Maybe a wine store isn't the best place for a child to play."

Rivien opened her mouth but then closed it again, biting her tongue in the process.

"Nugget, why don't you go back to the playroom. I'll come start a movie for you in a minute, make some microwave popcorn. You go get your stuffies all situated."

"Okay, Mama," Rita said, the injury forgotten. "But I want chocolate too."

"No, it's popcorn with movies. That's a healthy snack."

Rita fixed Rivien with her best stink eye, but then shrugged her shoulders, the pint-sized only child an adept mimic of the adults around her.

"Okay. I'll ask Baba," she said, as she made a dramatic turn and headed off to the small office that had been converted to a playroom.

"Thanks, Mom," Rivien said sarcastically.

"Listen. I am doing my best to entertain her, but today is her day off preschool, and yet here we are, watching you work on the store again."

"I didn't know this shipment was coming today. I wanted to take her to the playground, but it's pouring rain anyway. So I just need to get this wine out of the way for the next delivery, and then we can go upstairs and play."

"I thought you said that when you stopped being a doctor, your life was going to get simpler. Wasn't that the point?"

"Yes, Mom. That is the point. But it's hard to start a business. I was hoping it was going to go quicker than it is, but it isn't. I have to get things organized if I ever want to have a more normal life."

"You really think being a business owner is ever going to be an easy life?"

"I didn't say *easy*, I said *normal*. You really think being a doctor was a normal life? Do I need to remind you what happened?"

Marcia's eyes went dark. "You never need to remind me. You think you need to remind a mother that her oldest daughter almost died? Not once but twice? You think I need to be reminded of that?"

Oh, I'm not about to let you out-Jewish-mother-guilt-trip me. "No, just like I don't need to be reminded that my job almost took me away from Rita, forever. So you know what? I'm up for a little pain now, to change the future, our future. I need to do something different, something not life and death. Something where I don't always feel like I am wrong, even when I'm right. Can't you understand that?"

Marcia's eyes softened, as did Rivien's, a mirror of motherhood across generations. "Yes, honey, of course I can. It will be different challenges, that's all. Sure, no calls, no late nights at the hospital, but there will be other stresses. And who do you have to rely on?"

"I'll get staff, Mom, at least a few, someone good, once everything is set up."

"And when will that be? It's been six months since you closed your practice. A year since you got back from the north."

"I know. It's taking longer than I thought, or I hoped, anyway. But I'll get there. I want it to be right, I want to set us up for success. I know this year will be tough, but if we can open by the New Year, then I can work out the kinks before Rita starts kindergarten in the fall. Then I can have a routine that works for her."

"But what about money? I'm sure you'll be a success, but…it won't be medicine, will it. It will be a change."

"Mom, we weren't rich growing up on the farm, and I was fine. I'm fine, we're fine now. Rita and I love our place. And I know not everyone thinks living in an apartment above a store is the dream, but we love it. We can walk anywhere downtown. And Coulee Butte is getting better all the time, it's a fun way to live. I feel almost European."

"But the money. I mean, I know it's costing more than you thought to get up and going."

"You know? How?" Rivien said, already knowing the answer. She walked past Marcia toward the back, realizing she had not heard noise coming from the makeshift playroom in the last several minutes.

Marcia followed. "I mean, your sister mentioned something, is all. I think she worries too."

"Yeah, well, she doesn't have to. We don't all need to be as successful as Edi." Rivien wondered why attorney-client privilege didn't hold when your lawyer was your sister. She opened the door to the playroom to see Rita asleep on a large beanbag, mouth open, snoring gently, buried in a pile of stuffed animals.

"It's not that. She knows the settlement money won't go as far as we all hoped, to give you some breathing room."

Rivien closed the playroom door behind her. "Well, I only took that fucker's money, or I mean that fucking hate group's money, to drive them into the ground, so they couldn't try to use some fake-ass church status to spread their anti-choice rhetoric anymore."

"I know, I know, honey, don't get upset."

"But I am upset, Mom. I'm upset that everyone seems to think I'm crazy, like, 'Why would she leave such a lucrative career' and 'Why would she put her child through that?' I'm 'upset' because being a doctor is an impossible fucking job. You can never be good enough; the demands keep coming and coming. Haven't I earned the chance to do something else now? Don't I deserve it?"

Rivien was fighting hard to hold in the tears, but of course her own mother knew. Marcia hugged her, and Rivien rested her head on top of her mother's.

"Honey, I'm sorry, of course you do. And I know, if anyone can rise to this challenge, it's you. I really do know that. I want what's best for you, and for Rita. That's all I want. I hope this choice, this life, will give it to you."

"I think that's it, Mom. I don't think I ever really thought about my decision to be a doctor. It wasn't a choice, it was a challenge. I wanted to be the one that made it. Everyone and their dog thinks they can do our job now, all you need are some online courses or an internet connection. Let 'em."

"I know, honey. I know it's become too much. After such a long road in medicine, you've earned a break. And I trust you, your dad and I both do. Your sister too, she really does. We have your back, honey. And you know I will always be here to look after Rita, whenever you need me. She's the best thing in our lives. You've got this."

Rivien let herself sink into her mother. The weight of the last year, and her many hard years of sacrifice in medicine, were a burden she could not seem to shake. A cloak, which for many years had pulled her down, but also identified her to the world. A doctor. A healer. A commodity.

"I'm tired of being a doctor, Mom, tired of being *that* doctor, the one who was attacked for doing my job. I want to be Rita's mom, a regular mom, with a regular job."

"I understand, honey. I do. And you're almost there. I know you need to change, to push yourself. That didn't come from being a doctor; that's who you are. You wanted to have a baby, and you did. You made it happen, by yourself. And now look at you both. You can make this work, I really didn't mean to imply otherwise. I worry, that's what moms do. I know you know that too."

"I do, Mom, and thanks. And thanks for looking after Rita. We're lucky to have you. And Dad too when he can tear himself away from the farm."

Marcia took her daughter by the shoulders, looked up into her face, and smiled.

"Popcorn!" came the loud demand from the playroom.

"Popcorn what?" called Rivien.

"Popcorn pleeeease..." came the echo.

"Wonder if she even knew she fell asleep?" Marcia said.

"Doubtful. Eat, sleep, play. She's such a good kid. All right, let's get the snacks going and I'll put on a short show. Let me finish cleaning up and move these boxes, then let's go upstairs to the apartment. I want some playtime. We'll get a pizza and have a fun afternoon."

"Sounds like what we all need."

Rivien couldn't agree more.

CHAPTER 2

The next day, Marcia took Rita to the library for a children's concert and playtime while Rivien continued to work in the store, feeling less guilty now that Rita had other children to play with and an entire library of activities to explore. Rivien's store and the apartment she shared with Rita were in a renovated 1905 heritage building. The setup allowed Rivien to pop upstairs quickly to do laundry, pack lunches, or sneak in a little nap when needed. *No wonder I still haven't opened the store!* Today, without adorable but insistent interruptions, she was determined to finally master her cloud-based inventory system in preparation for actually stocking her shelves.

"Of course," Rivien said when her cell phone started ringing. Getting into a flow at her new job was continuing to prove a challenge. As she picked up the phone, the caller ID threw her back in time to the shambles that was her life last fall in northern Saskatchewan. A simple locum assignment that turned into a double murder and a town-wide conspiracy. The horrifying memory had not left her consciousness, and seeing the familiar name pop up on her call display brought a flush of warmth to her face but a chill to her soul. She thought about letting the call go to voice mail, but instead, knowing she'd only wonder what it was about, she answered.

"Hello," she said, quickly stopping herself from adding "this is Dr. Rivien," as had been her habit for so many years.

"Rivien, I'm so glad this is still your number. I was really hoping you hadn't changed it. It's been a long time. It's Karen Pinder, the medical examiner from Saskatchewan."

"Karen, it's nice to hear from you. Yeah, it's been a while. You're calling me on a Sunday, so I hope this is a personal call. What's up?" replied Rivien, hoping the note of dread she felt was not slipping into her voice. Why would Karen be calling now? Had they managed to piece together any of the identities of the unknown murderers from Palladium City? Was there going to be a trial? Any confirmation of guilt?

"Sorry, professional, actually. I'm on call this weekend. Listen, I have a favor to ask. I heard you retired from medicine, and I want to say good for you. You've been through enough. I totally get it."

"Thanks, I appreciate that. What can I do for you? Is this about Palladium? Did anything happen?"

"No, no. Nothing about that, fortunately, or unfortunately. I'm still not really sure how to feel about the way that whole mess was left. Actually, I moved to Alberta about six months ago, took an ME job here. I want to hire you as a contractor, as a coroner. With the opioid crisis still endemic, we are so short-staffed in the ME's office they are going to go back to using coroners, or ME's investigators, as they call them now. Anyway, I want to hire you."

"Thanks, Karen. That's nice of you to think of me, but I don't have a medical license anymore, no malpractice insurance. And I'm opening a wine store, so that's keeping me busy, but I'm loving it."

"Wow, a wine store? Now that's a departure. Good for you. But why a wine store?"

"I took some leave after Palladium. It was too much all piled on so shortly after the attack. But I don't do well with sitting still, so I started taking some wine classes online, then in person in the city for a few days here and there. I'd always liked wine but never realized how much there was to actually know about it. It's really fascinating."

"Well, it must be, to hold your attention."

"I think part of why I like it is it's so different from medicine. I like the history, the economics of it."

"And the wine…"

"Yes, of course, and the wine. Probably too much. I already know I have to be careful not to drink my profits. Anyway, I did a few more small locums, local stuff, office work. But my heart wasn't in it anymore. So I made the leap. Committed to the classes while Rita was on summer break. We went to the city a few weeks at a time, stayed with my sister, and I got some certifications. So yeah, here I am. Right now I'm struggling with the business side of things."

"Yeah, that has got to be tough. Such a huge change."

"Yes and no. I mean, it is, but it's still my business, so I feel like I have some control. That is a nice feeling."

The elusive dream of peace hung gently between the two doctors for a moment. They both sighed.

"I let my medical license go," Rivien continued. "I knew if I held on to it, I'd get dragged back in with requests for coverage, little admin jobs. I needed a clean break. I guess I can always go back if I need to, if this plan doesn't work. But for now, no license and no plans to jump through all those hoops again. So I am sorry I can't help you."

"Whoa, you don't get off the hook that easily. You don't need a license—you don't even need to be a doctor to do this job. There is a real mixed bag of backgrounds. Ex-cops, some nurses, I think we even have one investigator who has a bachelor's in anthropology or something. The investigators compile information, do paperwork, site visits if needed, some basic preparation possibly."

"So why can't you find people for that work, since you don't really need a health background? It must be a decent-paying job?" Rivien looked around the store, knowing that despite the settlement cushion, the bills would continue to pile up.

"We can find people, but I need someone like you, and that's the problem. I've got a set of cases that need someone with a doctor's brain. It's not patient care, so you don't need to be in the College, and you'd be a contractor so you would be covered by our liability umbrella. It isn't full-time or permanent, just for these cases."

Rivien hesitated. She had a lot of respect for Karen, who had been supportive and professional during their interactions last fall, and she believed her to be an ethical physician. Karen had fought hard for their marginalized victim last year even when some factions preferred to sweep the event under the rug.

"I don't know how I would work that with the store. I'm not even open yet and I really need to get the lead out. I want to be up and running in a few months, by the New Year."

"Well," Karen continued, undaunted, "I don't think this will take long; it's some extra money in your pocket, and a big help for me. And here's another thing: these cases are actually in your city, in Coulee Butte. I asked around before I called you, and made sure there wasn't a conflict, but I thought you'd be in the best position to understand what is happening there."

"Really? Are these overdose cases? I know there have been a lot lately, lots of people struggling after the pandemic."

Now it was Karen's turn to hesitate. "No, it's not that. These are actually inpatient hospital deaths, well, hospice deaths really, and there has been a complaint raised against a doctor. That's why I checked that you and he had never worked together. He's pretty new to the community, so you wouldn't have overlapped long. I think he came around the time of your attack, before you went to Palladium."

"A doc. Shit. Really? That's not good. But you said hospice. No offense, but people in hospice are pretty much expected to die."

"I know, I hear you, and that is exactly why I can't send another investigator; the level of situational understanding is not something they are going to be able to acquire right away. They wouldn't even know how to begin to approach this situation. So that is why I need you. You can work on this whatever hours you can, nights, days, whatever suits you. If you can take a little break from the store, we pay really well, and will pay by the hour. Record it. If you can swing this, I can get a contract ready for you today. I have the file with the cases and the complaint ready for you to review at the hospital, with a rep from the College."

"But what am I actually doing? I'm not a cop, so I can't charge anyone," said Rivien. "Last year, Justin reminded me all the time that I wasn't a cop."

"Are you guys still together?" Karen asked.

"Well, not really together, certainly not geographically. He got posted out to the Maritimes."

"Oh, man, really? That's too bad. Long distance is a bitch."

"Agreed. I mean, we're sort of trying it, but not really. I don't know. He offered to reject the posting, try to get posted closer to here."

"But…you…didn't want him to?"

"Sort of. I mean, I really like him, but our relationship started with the craziness of Palladium. I don't know if you can build a solid foundation on that. And with Rita, I need to be careful. I don't want someone coming into her life who will leave her. It seemed too fast. And the posting was a good one, only far away. I didn't want to make him choose and then regret he chose us."

"But you still talk?"

"Yes, fairly often. And I've been out there once to see him. It was great, actually. So great it made me sad I didn't tell him to stay. So I don't know what is going to happen. There is no one else right now, so we'll see how things go."

"Well, you don't need to be a cop on this one. You're simply fact gathering. I haven't even been able to make a finding of suspicious death in these cases, so I need someone to look more at the situation and the picture as a whole. You do what you think needs to be done, follow the situation as you see fit. There are some basic forms, but really, you are going to write a report of your actions and findings, and if there is even a whiff of anything criminal, we will kick it to the cops and you get to walk away. The ME gets all the death certificates, and in-hospital deaths are all coded one way, which is why we know about them. But even though the cops have heard rumblings, they only get formally involved if there is a finding of suspicion, and right now I can't clarify that without some more context."

"But you said there had been a complaint raised? Didn't that go through the cops? How else did you get flagged to even look into these hospice deaths more closely?"

"No, the complaint was about the physician. It went to the College of Physicians and Surgeons, who then sent it to us and the cops. But the cops are not going to move on it if there's nothing suspicious, and that really requires looking into the deaths themselves first, and that is on us."

"The College doesn't just forward complaints about patient care to the ME and the cops without looking into it first. Even if a doc made mistakes, that doesn't automatically make it criminal."

"The complaint went past indicating care errors, or poor judgment. There was at least a suspicion of more serious wrongdoing. There were some cases brought forward in the pandemic, angel of mercy type docs deciding who should die and when.

I think the College is on high alert; in other places medical administration has been roasted for not acting quickly enough when concerns are raised."

Despite her initial reluctance, Rivien was intrigued. Curiosity had always been both a constructive and a destructive part of her personality, and she couldn't turn it off. She also knew the money would be really helpful, and it's not like she'd be seeing patients; she was looking into charts and assessing what had already occurred. Although she'd be using her past skills and knowledge, she wasn't going down the slippery slope of medical familiarity. She would be a consultant, not a doctor, and maybe that could work. *Maybe.*

"Can I think about it?"

"You can, but only for the day," Karen replied. "I obviously need to get started on this. I'm thinking you could do all the chart reviews, maybe some interviews, whatever you would need in under a week, then you'd be done. We'd pay for all your time, including the report preparation, and you'd have official ID and also a release that covers your access to the materials you need. Think about it. Could you call me back by tomorrow morning at the latest?"

"Yes, I will. I need to talk to my mom, but if I can make it work, I'll let you know."

"Okay, I'm going to email you the standard contract right away anyway, so you can review the terms. I hope this will work. I know I can work with you, and I need your eyes on this."

Rivien thanked Karen for her trust and hung up. Was it worth it? Or should she persevere with her new life plan, selling wine and ignoring dead bodies?

CHAPTER 3

Rivien shook her head as she strode toward the doors of the hospital. *How exactly did I end up back here? Slippery slope,* she cautioned herself silently. The hospital looked like any other built in the heyday of provincial overspending; although those days were long gone, the decor of the hospital was an ongoing reminder. The 1980s mint and peach tiles were meant to be soothing, but they looked out of place with the garish new donor-appreciation wall with a huge TV screen that occupied one entire wall in the entryway. *Wonder what that cost?* No expense had been spared on the plethora of faceted glass bricks adorning every free space. The joke at the hospital had always been that the "Crystal Tower" was one tornado away from catastrophe. As she crossed the well-lit but dated lobby, she smiled at those she recognized and stopped to make the obligatory small talk with nurses she knew well.

"Wow, I wish I could retire in my forties," said one young nurse, who at two years into the job didn't seem to understand Rivien's position. "You're so lucky!"

Rivien winced. She hated being told she was lucky, even discounting her brush with death. "Well, I wouldn't say lucky. I mean, I worked hard for years, and getting shot because of my job wasn't exactly lucky."

The young nurse's face fell, and Rivien silently kicked herself for being oversensitive.

"I'm sorry," the nurse said.

"No, I'm sorry," said Rivien. "I know what you mean. And you know what, I actually do feel lucky. It's not easy here. I get where you're coming from."

The young nurse smiled before moving on. Rivien hoped she had made up for her snarky blunder, but she knew she would probably be talked about at the nurses' station later that day.

Next came a physiotherapist with whom Rivien had a personal and professional relationship; their daughters attended the same preschool. For her, Rivien even sat for a moment, sharing a coffee, savoring that her hospital mission today was not really time sensitive, at least not to the degree to which she was accustomed.

"So do you miss it?" her friend asked.

"Miss what? The stress? The lack of support or recognition?" Rivien said with a smirk.

"No, smart-ass, I mean do you miss the helping?"

Rivien was silent for a moment, a rarity. "Of course I do, when I was actually helping. But I don't need to tell you the system is broken. It's an awful feeling, letting people down. But I feel it even more, now that I up and quit."

"Give yourself a break, Rivien. You did plenty, and it's not all on you. Other people, the system, they need to solve their own problems."

"You're right. I know. And I know what happened to me actually made some difference."

"Well, that's something."

"Yeah. The health authority of course tried to take credit for it, you know, all their hard work to improve the provision of women's health. Such a crock of shit. They don't do anything until they think they look bad."

"You and I and anyone who works here knows it. But isn't it still better than the alternative. I mean, it might be disingenuous, but at least it got money into programs and got women more of the help they need."

"You're right, of course. I'm just bitter. And I need to let it go; otherwise, what was the point of even leaving? I could have stayed here and bitched."

"Hey, after the pandemic, isn't bitching the way to get things done? Complain louder than everyone else and get your way?"

"Feels like that. Hence why I'm opening a wine shop!"

"Hey, you supply the wine, I'll listen to you complain all day long."

"Deal!" Rivien left her friend with a brief hug but also a slight sadness. *Maybe I haven't "gotten over it" as well as I thought. Slippery slope.* Not just the pull of the work, but the pull of the hurt as well. Medicine was like a toxic boyfriend: she had left him, so why the hell was he still on her mind?

Of course, it was hardly surprising she'd be thinking of medicine while at the hospital for Karen's short-term gig. Rivien had calculated that a week's worth of part-time work would bring in about three thousand dollars. Karen had bumped up her hourly rate because of Rivien's advanced training. Rivien had told Karen that she thought the work would be interesting, but she told herself it was more about the money. Maybe that was true and maybe it wasn't.

As promised, Karen had sent the needed charts and investigative reports to the hospital. The deaths at issue arose in the hospice, and, in Coulee Butte, the only hospice was located in another area of town in a separate facility. But for now, the hospital was a convenient meeting place, since the College of Physicians and Surgeons was sending an investigator too. Karen had advised Rivien that the College's associate registrar was meant to work with Rivien, a prospect at which she was less than thrilled.

Rivien herself had thankfully never had a significant run-in with the College, and now she fell outside of their mandate, or their control. But the College was still the College, and it was the main regulatory body for all doctors in the province. Rivien's estimation of any medical College had soured after her northern locum, and she had minced no words discussing that with Karen when Rivien had called her back to accept the job.

"Don't you remember what the College was like in Saskatchewan last year? They swept all the horrible things that doctor did under the rug."

"Well, he was murdered, Rivien, it's not like they could sanction him after the fact." Rivien liked Karen, but what a piss-off she was always so reasonable!

"I know, I know. But I think the predators often get away with it, even when they are alive. I mean the Colleges talk a good game about monitoring physicians, but then why are there so many issues, so many bad ones?"

"Well, that is what we are trying to do here, Rivien, find out if this one is a bad one or not."

"So you're telling me that I can't just complain about the College and then do nothing to try to help with a solution? That is what I like to do." Rivien chuckled.

"No, you don't," Karen said. "I know you, and I knew I'd get you interested in this problem. I knew you'd help me."

"Damn it, I need to stop being so predictable."

Karen's last statement had stuck with Rivien, and she recalled it now. "You may be a lot of things, Rivien, but predictable isn't really one of them."

CHAPTER 4

Rivien was to meet the College rep in the shared offices at the hospital that were made available to visiting lecturers or locums. Rivien's entry scan card still worked; apparently no one had realized she didn't have privileges in the facility anymore. She even went and checked the mail room, where her box was not only still labeled but still accruing hospital announcements and magazine offers. After binning all but the one old emergency record that actually required her signature before filing, she headed to the communal office wing. It was located in an isolated hall on the sixth floor, a site that had previously been a patient care location, now unfortunately not used for that purpose due to lack of staffing.

She used her scan card to access the sixth floor in the elevator and headed down the hall to a conference room. As she pulled open the door, she realized she was late to the party. Sitting at the desk was a woman in her mid- to late fifties. She had graying dark hair cut short and olive skin set off by her bright red blazer and delicate but copious gold jewelry. She was fine-boned and very thin, but not underfed. More like a delicate bird. Rivien was slim but next to her felt like a giant occupying the entirety of the doorway where she had stopped. The other woman already had a large pile of paperwork in front of her.

"Hi, I'm Rivien, I'm the ME's investigator. Are you from the College?"

"Yes, hi. I'm Priyana. Dr. Chapan. I'm an associate registrar with the College."

"Oh, good. Karen, Dr. Pinder, told me to meet you here so we could look at things *together*." The slightest hint of snark crept into Rivien's voice as she nodded toward the already-open papers. She wondered how Priyana would react to her mildly passive-aggressive comment and didn't even feel bad about laying it out that way. It was the first step in the investigation, feeling out the person with whom she would be working.

"Yes, excellent," answered Priyana with no tone of defense, no note of judgment—not really even with any apparent recognition of Rivien's tone. Rivien decided that was acceptable, even desirable. "Sorry to get started without you, I was too curious to wait," said Priyana as her dark eyes sparkled. Rivien decided this woman was likely older than she'd thought, maybe even late sixties or early seventies, but her brightness made her appear much younger, a doctor near the end of her career but still eager to contribute. She was the type of woman Rivien's own mother would call "vibrant," a compliment of the highest order from one woman of substance to another.

"No worries, I'm intrigued too," Rivien replied, always a bit surprised but grateful there were still keen doctors in the world.

"I understand you are a retired physician, correct? Now contracted by the ME to help with this case?" asked Priyana.

"Yes, I let my license go earlier this year," Rivien answered, looking for any sign of recognition or concern in Priyana's face. "I know the ME a bit personally. She thought she needed some doctor eyes on the ME investigation side of things."

"Agreed. Any time concerns are raised about a physician, things can get very complicated. It's a balance between pouncing on any criticism, often unfounded, versus not doing enough to protect the public."

"I hear you. I guess I'm hoping there isn't anything bad going on here, but I know hoping it is so and making it so aren't the same thing. Got to watch out for that premature diagnostic closure," Rivien quipped.

"Yes," Priyana said, smiling. "I am glad you are here. I am sure your skills will be a great asset. I'm really hoping we can get to the bottom of this unfortunate situation quickly."

Rivien, who had always been quick to form judgments, although not always correctly, felt like Priyana was giving off good vibes, but pressed on to feel her out a bit more.

"Have you ever been to Coulee Butte before? To our little hospital?"

"No, can't say as I've had the pleasure. I just drove in today, but it seems like a very nice city."

"Yeah, it is. The hospital can be a bit strange. It's a small enough place that everyone knows everyone's business."

"Yes, but in our line of inquiry, that could be a benefit. Not gossip, of course, but…directions, leads to follow, let's say."

Rivien nodded. Maybe having a partner would be okay.

Priyana continued, "It's a bit sad this floor was closed. I can see it used to be patient rooms. A few rooms have been turned into a simulation lab, but the rest is offices. Were the patient care beds not needed?"

"Oh, they were needed, but no staff to run them. This actually used to be the hospice floor, when the hospital had one."

"Well, these deaths we are looking into, they occurred in the hospice, did they not?"

"Yes, but that is over at a different facility, St. Michael's. It's across the river."

"But the physician, the one we are looking into, he has privileges here, doesn't he?"

"I assume so. Probably at both facilities. St. Michael's isn't a hospital, it's short-stay community rehab beds and the hospice wing. It's run by Sacrament Health."

"Ah yes, of course, that makes sense."

"Well, if you believe having a publicly funded Catholic health organization running facilities in tandem with the general provincial ones makes sense."

Rivien hadn't meant to blurt out her long-standing frustration with the incestuous relationship between health and religion. She awaited Priyana's response.

"Yes, that is still very strange to me. It was not that way in the province I worked in previously. It certainly adds complexity, I'm sure."

Well, thought Rivien, *may as well double down and really tell her how you feel.* "Not just complexity—ethical issues. Catholic facilities, even though they operate with public tax dollars, will not permit abortions or medical assistance in dying in their facilities, at least not in this province."

"Yes, I have seen news stories about that. It is very distressing, as I am not sure how they can believe, or say, that they are practicing patient-centered care."

"Exactly!" Rivien said, emboldened by agreement. "And it's not about the individual people. There are a lot of people that work there, or are even from the church, that don't feel that way. It's the institution, a disembodied organization that somehow acts like it has more rights than the patients...or the staff. That is what is so frustrating."

"How is this still going on in this day and age?"

"It's some old law that set up the two systems, like in the schools, but no one is willing to change it, to question it. I mean, if they weren't taking public dollars, I'd say they could do what they want, but that's not the case. Unfortunately, after this floor closed, the Catholic hospice became the only option in town."

"Well, I did notice on my way here that this public hospital still has a little chapel, if I'm not mistaken. We don't see that in the city anymore; they are called 'quiet spaces' now."

"Yup," said Rivien. "Ours is still a chapel, and I think at last count it was three Jesuses, two Marys, and about a half dozen crosses in there. I actually brought it up once, to hospital management, after I literally tripped over one of our Muslim docs praying in a back hallway, since he had nowhere else to go. They told me, 'It's nondenominational. Protestants are welcome to use it too.' "

"Oh my. Did you take it any further?"

"Honestly, no, I didn't. Quite frankly, I watched my mom get called a Christ-killer behind her back when she dared to request that a six-foot Jesus be removed from my public school when I was a kid. She was the first Jew in our town. I didn't think anyone else would listen."

"I'm sorry that happened. And it's not okay. I'll think on it, maybe I can make some suggestions."

"I appreciate that. We've still got a long way to go."

"Very true. Now I hate to change the subject, as I really do appreciate your insights on the local context here, but I think you'll see some of these issues are reflected in the complaint letter that the College received. It makes more sense to me now that I understand more clearly that the involved facility is a faith-based institution."

"Okay, now you've got my attention."

"Well, then, let's start digging."

CHAPTER 5

The first document the pair looked at was the original College complaint. It had been filed by a Mr. Gerald Strong, who gave his position as facility manager, St. Michael's.

"Ah, see, I didn't really catch the 'Saint' part on my initial read," Priyana said. "I didn't really think that a city this size would have a Sacrament facility, especially not providing the only hospice care."

"Yeah, we still have community palliative care available, but the only facility-based care is there. You gotta be okay with spending your final days surrounded by crosses."

"Well, certainly not everyone is okay with that, are they?"

"I've heard of at least a few who aren't, or weren't. But of course Sacrament doesn't hear about the people who refused to go there, so they think there's nothing wrong."

"Before you retired from medicine, did you work there at all?"

"No. I never did palliative care or seniors' care. I did do sexual reproductive health, but my services would not be welcome in that facility."

"Yes, I see now. We'll see how this letter strikes you, then."

There was only one copy of all the documents, so Rivien and Priyana literally put their heads together and read through the complaint.

> *Dear Sirs and Madams;*
>
> *I take no pleasure in writing to you, but I believe strongly in the duty of every health-care administrator to stand up, to speak out, and to sometimes take uncomfortable action to protect those for whom we care. I am the site manager at St. Michael's Health Facility, a hospice and rehabilitation care center in Coulee Butte, Alberta. Our facility is home to a 12-bed hospice unit and I take great pride in the compassionate and high-level care we provide to residents in their final days.*
>
> *I am sad to say that in the last two weeks I have become increasingly concerned about the care provided by one of the facility's contract physicians, Dr. Josh Landry. Dr. Landry provides general palliative care on a rotating basis for our residents and is a family physician in our town. I have always found Dr. Landry to be a highly competent and skilled family physician, but recently I have had reason to become concerned.*
>
> *In the last two weeks, two patients on our unit have died suddenly. I am sure that patients dying on a palliative floor does not sound out of the ordinary, but nurses have raised concerns in two instances, and I have looked into the issue myself before approaching you and local medical leadership. Both of the patients involved had terminal diagnoses (I can share demographics at an appropriate time and as directed*

under appropriate authorization), but their deaths were not thought to be imminent. However, both patients in fact succumbed suddenly, very proximal in time to a visit by Dr. Landry.

One patient died while Dr. Landry was on rounds in his room, despite having been conversing with the nurse within the half-hour. A second patient was found deceased mere moments after Dr. Landry left the building one morning, despite the patient having just ordered a specific breakfast item they were waiting to be brought up from the kitchen. Although our patients may certainly succumb to their disease quickly, what raises concern for myself and my nurses is that both these patients had expressed a strong belief in God, and had resisted any medication administration they felt crossed the boundary between controlling pain and hastening their death, even as an unintended consequence. Dr. Landry had verbally expressed frustration with this approach and felt he was being forced to "harm" the patients by holding back on treatments that could ease their suffering.

Again, I take no pleasure in reporting this matter to you, but family of both patients are distraught as neither patient had family present when they passed. I do hope that a reasonable explanation is found in these cases, but I did not feel it was right to keep this information and my concerns to myself. Of course, as these were at the time considered "expected" deaths, no autopsies were ordered. The most recent of these deaths occurred over a week ago. I regret it took me several days to learn of the nurses' concerns and to do a brief investigation of the matter.

I thank you very much for your attention. I believe strongly that patients for whom we are caring with the goal of comfort are as important as those patients whose goal remains cure. As facility manager, I have suspended Dr. Landry's privileges at our facility only until this matter can be addressed. I do hope you will take my concerns seriously and pursue an investigation of this matter.

Sincerely,
Gerald Strong

As Rivien finished reading the complaint, Priyana, clearly the superior speed reader and slightly ahead, was already shuffling through the remaining pile of paperwork.

"So, what did you think?" asked Priyana.

"Well, Karen had said you guys were interested because there was some suspicion this was an angel of mercy doctor, killing patients they thought needed to go, even if that wasn't what the patient wanted. The letter seems to confirm that is the concern."

"But what you said, about this being a faith-based hospice, adds a bit to this, because they would not have allowed medical assistance in dying to happen there. Is there a chance that it was actually the patients secretly asking for MAID and this Dr. Landry was complying, as a way to get around the organizational restriction?"

"I guess that is possible, especially if the family was against MAID. If the patients didn't feel they could speak up to family or the institution, this may have been the only way for them to get it. Dr. Landry would still be in trouble, but it wouldn't be as bad as the alternative."

"Well, let's see what else we have here," said Priyana. "Looks like Dr. Pinder was able to supply copies of both patients' death certificates, and the College arranged for copies of the charts for both patients to be provided for our review. We can also consult the provincial electronic record."

"This seems fast to me, to get all this put together," Rivien said. "I was surprised the ME even got involved, solely based on a College complaint. Aren't those things pretty common? Disgruntled patients? Docs complaining about each other?" Rivien was still thinking there was only smoke here, no evidence of a real fire at all.

"Agreed. I asked about that too. Apparently, like the College and hospital administrators, the ME has been put on notice to have a high suspicion for any irregularity in any MAID deaths, given the changes in the law and the likely future changes around mental illness, advance directives, and the like."

"But these weren't MAID deaths, or not formal ones that would have the associated paperwork at the ME's office," countered Rivien. "Even that guy Gerald said they didn't raise any flags initially. ME was likely not even contacted, just provided the death certificate afterward as is standard protocol."

"I think when this complaint came across the College's desk, they reached out to the ME right away. The College has the same low threshold for ensuring MAID is not tarnished or left to run wild, and so this concern flagged them to contact the ME urgently. Although these aren't MAID deaths, the College knows that Dr. Landry has privileges at the public hospital as a MAID provider."

"So…because he provides a service that some people, some doctors, think is immoral, it's okay to put him under a stronger microscope than any other physician?" Rivien could feel the hairs stand up on the back of her neck. *Singled out for sticking one's neck out? Where have I heard this before?*

"Although the College won't say it, yes, I am afraid that is the case," Priyana said. "Although we are anxious to find no wrongdoing, we have to ensure it is looked into in order to keep public trust in our ability to regulate physicians in this province."

"I'm not going to lie, Priyana. I'm not sure how we are going to determine if there is really something wrong here, or if the complaint from St. Mike's is just another symptom of physicians being expected to be infallible, when we clearly aren't."

"I hear you, I do. This is obviously something the College hears all the time. And believe me, we know there can be mistakes, and that is okay. People and doctors make mistakes. And we can help communicate that, when it is warranted. But if there was intent here, to override patient autonomy to—quite frankly—commit murder, we obviously need to look into that."

"But maybe it was intent to bend the stupid rules and help a patient, like you said—couldn't that be possible?"

"Yes, it could. And unfortunately, I have confirmed that one patient from the complaint was already cremated, and the other one buried, so I share your concern that this stack of papers isn't going to hold the answers we need."

The women sat on that for a while. Although Rivien was not the one policing another physician, how was she going to decide what the evidence might be for reopening a case when there weren't even bodies to examine? Would the ME seriously consider exhuming a palliative patient? She had heard of cases of health-care workers who killed patients for years on end before finally being caught. She really hoped she was not stumbling into the center of such a shitstorm, but she figured that was why both the College and the ME were jumping on this.

Priyana looked over and gently placed her hand on top of Rivien's.

"We are not the police. We are here to get the ball rolling. MAID is an important medical procedure, it matters, and I respect a patient's right to choose for themselves. I can tell you do too. We are not here to condemn the practice, but it is in no one's best interest if we let it even appear that medically assisted death can get muddled with euthanasia."

Rivien squeezed Priyana's hand. It was small, much smaller than her own, almost like a child's, and it comforted Rivien, the same as holding her own child's. It felt accepting, lacking judgment—a beautiful invitation, not to be perfect, but to do her best. She felt that way every time she held Rita as well.

"Okay, so what do we do first?" asked Rivien.

"Well, I don't know about you, but I could definitely go for some brunch."

"Sounds fantastic. I know a place we can strategize."

"And drink coffee. Definitely more coffee."

"I thought you were my kinda lady, Priyana. Let's go!"

CHAPTER 6

Rivien's favorite brunch spot near the hospital was an adorable café with pink umbrellas on a small patio. Rivien ordered shakshuka and Priyana followed suit. As they dug into the spicy tomato sauce and piled their eggs onto dipped sourdough chunks, they formulated a plan.

"I'm thinking we need to go over to St. Mike's," Rivien said. "Karen made sure I had some ID and a letter from the ME's office detailing my role, so we should head over there and see if we can speak to any nurses familiar with the complaint. Maybe look at the layout, see if anyone has any idea what may have caused the deaths, specifically."

"I do think we need to do that," agreed Priyana, "but College policy would be to speak to the physician involved very early in the investigation, let them give us their side of the story, not only out of respect but also to have it on record. Often, we then find facts down the line that either support or refute their version of events. It pretty much sets the stage for how the investigation will turn out, and what kind of cooperation or contrition we can expect."

"Okay, I can go with that. It's not like we're showing our hand. This happened a few weeks ago, and Landry isn't working at the Sacrament facility now anyway, so it's not like he could remove any evidence at this point."

"Agreed. He received an email notification of the College's receipt of the complaint with a formal copy following in the mail, so he knows the complaint has been made; that is College policy. I am less sure if he knows the ME is investigating these deaths. This is still a coroner issue, but he may be more surprised to see you and learn your role. Might not be a bad thing, make him realize the seriousness."

"Okay, let's start with him and then go to the site, set up a meeting with Mr. Strong, and see if anyone has any actual idea, or better yet evidence, of what they think happened."

"I'll give Dr. Landry a call to see if we can set a time to meet with him. I have his contact details."

As Priyana stood and left the table for a minute to make the call, Rivien checked her own phone. An alert had come through the app the preschool used to show parents what their kids were up to in class. When Rivien opened it, up popped pictures of the whole class of kids out in the yard with giant bubbles, enjoying the very pleasant early fall day. Rivien smiled as she thumbed through the photos until she found one of Rita, her dark hair glistening with a mix of sunshine and bubble slime; her eyes were squeezed tight with a smile and laugh you could almost hear through the photograph.

"Is that your daughter?" Priyana asked. "Sorry, didn't mean to snoop."

"Not at all. Yeah, her name is Rita."

"How old is she?"

"Four. This is from her preschool. Looks like they're having a blast."

"I have a grandson. They live in Toronto, though. He is in kindergarten. I wish he was closer, so I could see him more often. But as much as technology frustrates me sometimes, it does allow more contact, doesn't it?" she said, gesturing to Rivien's phone.

"Yep. Definitely helps, on days I am working, to have my little Nugget break."

"What are you doing for work now? I mean, when you are not being an investigator?"

"This is a one-off. I hope. I'm actually opening a wine store. I mean I'm getting close to opening it."

"Really? Such a departure. Good for you. When I left my practice, I couldn't quite give up medicine, at least not completely. I taught for a little while, and then moved to the College. They'll probably have to drag me from the place. I would go crazy sitting at home. I don't know how to do anything else."

"Yeah, I definitely don't 'do nothing' well, but I am glad to try my hand at something outside of medicine."

"Well, I am glad Dr. Pinder convinced you to work on this case. I have never really done an investigation like this, with the ME, I mean. I am glad we can be a team."

"Me too. I had some craziness last fall, when I was on a locum up north. A doctor and a pharmacist were murdered, and I was the only doctor in the town. There was a cop who came to help and the whole thing went pear-shaped. The entire town was in on it. It was wild. I'm really hoping this is going to be more...sane."

"I remember reading about that, the murders. I had no idea you were involved. Is that how Dr. Pinder knew you? I had heard she was a recent import from Saskatchewan."

"Yes, that is the connection."

"Well, then, I too hope this partnership is nothing like that experience!"

Rivien nodded and asked, "Were you able to get a hold of Dr. Landry?"

"Yes, he said he'd be ready to meet us in forty-five minutes, at his office."

"Wow, that's good. Didn't he have patients?"

"He was fairly curt on the phone, but told me he had a short day booked and had canceled patients once he got the College notification."

"If we can see him now, depending how long that takes, maybe we can get to Sacrament today yet too. I'm hoping to get my whole part of this process wrapped up fairly quickly, since I still have lots to do at the store."

"Let's see what Dr. Landry has to say. Once we finish our coffees, of course."

CHAPTER 7

Dr. Landry opened his office door to them after one knock from Priyana. He was a youngish man, maybe a few years older than Rivien, late forties. He was attractive but in a somewhat scruffy way. He had long hair—shaggy would be the best word—but it suited him, sort of like a dirty-blond Keanu Reeves. He had three-day stubble and was wearing well-fitting jeans and a gray scrub top with his name embroidered on the chest. On his feet were Birkenstock sandals with no socks. Rivien could never understand why a doctor working around bodily fluids would want to be barefoot in leather Jesus-booties. He smiled quite warmly and waved them in. It had been his name alone on the placard on his door, indicating this was a solo practice. No secretary or medical assistant was present. Dr. Landry waved them to waiting room chairs, of which there were only six, rather than taking them back to an office.

"Sorry, it's a small place and my office is a mess. It's easier to meet out here, if you are okay with that. We're on our own." He locked the door behind them as they chose seats.

"Thanks for meeting with us on such short notice. I know no one is excited to get a visit from the College," Priyana said kindly.

"Actually, I am glad you're here. I want to get this mess figured out, get back to the hospice. Not let one malcontent jeopardize the rest of my practice any further. And I'm sorry, but are you from the College too?" Dr. Landry asked, addressing Rivien.

"No. I'm sorry. I mean, I'm Rivien Gilrie, Dr. Gilrie. I am a medical examiner's investigator. I have been asked to work with the College on investigating the two deaths that occurred at St. Michael's. I am here gathering information to submit to the ME to consider. I don't work for the police or anything," she added.

"Okay. I wasn't expecting that. Is it normal for the ME to get involved in a College complaint? I have never heard of this before."

"No, I will be honest," replied Priyana, "it is not common."

"I didn't do anything wrong. Those people were in palliative care. I know that Gerald has a chip on his shoulder about me, but I didn't think he would stoop so low."

"The decision was not made by Mr. Strong. When a complaint comes to the College, you have a right to read the complaint, as it was forwarded to you, but Mr. Strong's involvement ended after that. It was the College's decision to alert the ME. We have made absolutely no finding of responsibility or wrongdoing. This process simply allows us to gather all required information with hopefully minimal impact to you and your practice, Dr. Landry."

"I am not sure I totally believe that," said Dr. Landry hesitantly, "but okay. Don't really see as I have much choice. I want to get this over with. And please, call me Josh."

"Thank you, Josh," replied Rivien. "I really do want to stress that I am not working for the police. The ME wanted a doctor's eyes on this, rather than a regular investigator. She hoped I would be in a better position to understand your…situation."

"You used to be a doctor here, right? In town? I know I've heard your name before, but I don't think I ever met you in person."

"Yes, I was, and no, I don't think we crossed paths, but it's nice to meet you now."

Josh gave a small smile and turned to Priyana. "I'm really not surprised about the complaint, to be honest, although I'm pissed Gerald is using two natural deaths to try to bring it forward, lend gravitas. I thought he would just complain about the way I managed patients or that I was telling them about their rights, even in the hospice."

"Can you be more specific?" prompted Priyana, followed by the age-old family medicine oral exam classic: "Can you tell me more?"

"I'm one of the docs that does MAID in Coulee Butte. It's not a secret at this point, pretty much anyone remotely involved knows. There's only a handful of us, and I am the most involved. But some people are bothered by the fact that I do both MAID and palliative care; they think they should be separate. And then you have Sacrament. Their policy is that no MAID provisions can occur in their facilities, and they only begrudgingly allow MAID discussions or assessments. They got forced into that by the legislation about a year ago. But still no provisions. Like the building itself should have conscientious objection rights, never mind the providers. You know about that, right?" he said as he turned to stare directly at Rivien. "That's why I recognize your name. You were the doc who got shot for doing the abortions."

Rivien glanced at Priyana when Josh said the word *shot*, but she saw no shock in her eyes, only sadness, making it clear to Rivien that Priyana had known who she was, her provenance, from the moment they met.

Rivien nodded slightly, and Josh continued. "It's one thing with actual providers. I understand individual doctors, nurses, not being involved because of their personal beliefs. I support choice for everyone. You don't want someone doing this work if they don't believe in it; that wouldn't be good for anyone involved. So it's not about that. But for the building, the organization, that has no skin in the game to get a say? I'm so done with it."

"So you believe Mr. Strong's complaint was…retaliation for your professional beliefs?" asked Priyana.

"I know I was getting pretty vocal about my frustrations, even wrote an article for the paper, but things were getting worse so I sent a formal complaint to the provincial health authority and the premier's office. I even tried to track down their funding stream because it makes no sense to me. I mean, in this day and age, why do we have a separate Catholic health system, funded with public money? The facility, Sacrament, will make a palliative patient, in the last hours of their life, get packed up in an ambulance and driven across town to the hospital or a long-term care facility, sometimes even directly to the family room at the funeral home, just to get their MAID provision. Even during the pandemic, when everyone else was sacrificing and trying not to spread disease to vulnerable people in facilities, they still forced those people onto stretchers and out into the cold rather than have the nurse and me bring all our own supplies and do the provision in their own room."

Rivien hadn't realized how bad it had been. She knew MAID was not permitted in the facility, the same as abortion was barred in Catholic facilities, but the thought of packing up a dying patient to move them for the last hour of their life was pretty unconscionable, and in absolutely no conceivable way could it be called patient-centered care. She wanted to share her thoughts out loud but held her tongue in the guise of objectivity.

"I knew of course that Gerry was pissed at me. He's a friggin' deacon or something in the church, and runs that hospice like it's an actual church. We get so few people of other faiths here, or those we do have choose not to have their deaths occur surrounded by Our Mother Mary hanging from every wall. So they get away with it. Because no one, certainly not the government or the public health authority, will stand up to them."

"But this complaint was about specific deaths," Rivien interjected. "Mr. Strong said these patients certainly were not MAID patients."

"I know he didn't include names in the complaint, only that there were two concerns, but I bet I can guess which ones, because they were the only ones that occurred during my last two weeks at the facility. Many of my patients from that time are still there, I'm just not allowed to see them. Had to give my week to another doc." Josh had not raised his voice throughout the account; he had spoken rapidly, yet calmly, probably well versed in having to rationalize his particular practice to outsiders.

As Rivien was considering what questions to ask Josh, Priyana shared the patient names in question, and Josh confirmed he was aware of those cases and had been right in his guess.

"So why would Mr. Strong believe that there was anything abnormal about those deaths?" Rivien asked.

"Both patients were alert before their deaths, which of course can happen on a palliative ward. One, Mrs. Gardens, was in terrible pain but was refusing narcotics or sedatives because she wanted to die 'naturally,' in her words. The other, Mr. Baskins, died while I was in the room. It was actually really sudden—in midsentence he gasped and got stiff for a second, then died. I called the nurse but it's not like we're coding these people. They're all comfort level of care. But yes, even I was a bit taken aback on that one. Must have been a sudden heart attack. Anyway, the nurse that was on that day goes to the same church as Mr. Baskins, Mrs. Gardens, and Gerry Strong. I know because I've seen them holding hands and praying over patients. That is all fine and well if that is what the patient wants. But I think Gerry comes to the floor sometimes and prays for people when they are asleep. I mean, maybe not everyone wants that, but that thought would never cross his mind."

"So I guess it goes without saying," said Priyana, "that you deny any wrongdoing in the death of these patients and that, to your assessment, they were natural deaths."

"Yes, of course, I didn't do a thing to them. They just died."

Priyana thanked Josh and stood up, indicating to Rivien they were done with this stage of the interview. Rivien racked her brain to think of anything else she should ask Josh, since Priyana had already covered "Did you do it?"

"We have some more inquires to make. You will be provided with written documentation on any College findings or direction, and I will also be in touch personally if we have further questions," Priyana said, handing Dr. Landry one of her cards. The College would of course inform him of the outcome, but that could take a year. Other physicians would likely be asked to audit the charts of the involved cases and submit any findings. All of this took time. Rivien was hoping her work would be completed by the end of the week.

As they were about to leave, Rivien asked, "What is the nurse's name? The one that goes to the church?"

"Margaret. Pike. You can't miss her. Still wears a white nursing hat and I swear to God a crucifix that would put your average rapper to shame."

Rivien smiled, conjuring the image, as they closed the office door.

CHAPTER 8

Priyana and Rivien carpooled to St. Michael's, leaving Priyana's car at the Medical Arts building near the hospital. Rivien was familiar with the town and even knew how to score free parking near the hospice site. As Rivien went to step out of the car, Priyana stopped her.

"Can we talk for a minute? Before we go in."

"Sure, do you want to discuss a plan?"

"Well, yes, but no, that isn't what I mean. I feel I need to address what Dr. Landry said, about you being the doctor who was shot."

"Yeah, I could see that you already knew that, when he said it."

"I am sorry I did not bring it up before. I didn't want you to think that was all people thought about you."

"I appreciate that. I'm trying to move past it, and being away from medicine has definitely helped. I don't have to go back to the office, or really think about the kind of cases that put me in that position."

"But what about being here, at this facility? Dr. Landry suggested you would feel the same as he does about religious health-care institutions, because your work would not have been supported either, just like MAID. I can see his point."

"Well, yeah, I'm trying hard to let it go but yes, it does still frustrate me. The stigma around our work puts us in jeopardy. Josh's hospital privileges, my life."

"I hear you, so I need to ask. Do you think you can look at this objectively? I am not accusing you of anything, but I can see why this may be hard for you and for your recovery from the trauma. You don't have to come in. I can get copies of charts, share the outcomes of my interviews. Whatever is best for you."

Rivien paused for a moment before she spoke. She knew her normal response would be to snap back, get her guard up at the subtle suggestion that she was not qualified or suited for the job. But she didn't feel that need with Priyana. She was not fighting judgment, she was receiving support.

"I really appreciate that, I do. But you know what, I'm glad I get to look into this. Of course I do hope Dr. Landry did nothing wrong, but I know it isn't my call. I'm gathering the info."

"So you'll be okay to go into the hospice?"

"Oh yeah. When you're the only Jewish family in a very small town, you get pretty used to being the invisible minority and having to adapt to your surroundings. I'm not saying I'm not gonna shake my head a few times, but I can do it. Trust me, even a sinner like me won't catch on fire as I cross the threshold. At least I hope not!"

"Excellent. I like a sense of humor. This job—any job in medicine—would be intolerable without it," Priyana said as they climbed out of the car. "Let's go meet the big man, then, and I don't mean him," she added, gesturing to a ten-foot-tall white marble Jesus blocking their path to the front door.

"If you mean Mr. Strong, then I am anxious to see what he says. I think your decision not to call him and give him a heads-up was a good idea," Rivien said. "There is very little element of surprise in this town; everyone basically knows everyone's business all the time."

"Yes, and if we're lucky, maybe we can find Nurse Pike, or a few of the other nurses, and chat with them some before their boss catches on."

The hospice building was old, built long before the current hospital. There had been additions over the years, but the three-story brick main structure persevered. The grounds were gorgeously kept, with a closely trimmed lawn and a plethora of flowers adorning the beds flanking the front steps. A small sign proclaimed the exuberant display the work of the St. Michael's Ladies Auxiliary. Once in the facility, they took the elevator to the third floor, all of which was occupied by the hospice; the first two floors held long-term care and support beds. The walls, as Rivien had expected, were adorned with crosses and also calming prints of nature scenes, the frames often marked with tiny plaques commemorating the donor, or the loved one in whose name the art had been donated. The building was cool, even in the warm fall, and smelled clean and sanitary. Rivien and Priyana approached the nursing station in the hospice and introduced themselves, showing their credentials and letters of introduction.

"Ummm…I, I need to get the charge nurse," stammered the unit clerk. Rivien smiled to herself. *Guess the "fuzz" doesn't show up here regularly.* The charge nurse was immediately summoned and everyone in the nursing station seemed instantly on edge.

"We are following up on a complaint made to the College of Physicians and Surgeons."

The charge nurse was not placated by Priyana's explanation.

"Well, I am calling Gerry, I mean Mr. Strong. The facility manager," she said. "You will have to speak to him about this matter."

"Of course," replied Priyana, not giving away any disappointment that their element of surprise had not lasted long.

Rivien and Priyana stayed near the desk while the charge nurse went back to the report room to place the call in private. When she returned, she said, "He is off-site currently but is on his way back. He wishes he had been advised ahead of your visit."

"No worries," said Rivien. "Any chance Nurse Pike is on shift today? Could we maybe speak to her while we wait?"

The naming of a specific nurse started a twitter in the nursing station. "That is not possible. You need to speak to Mr. Strong first."

Despite the charge nurse's dictate, from inside the buzzing hive stepped an older and very upright woman who stated loudly, "I am she. Come this way, please, and we can speak." Before the charge nurse could protest, Margaret Pike signaled for Priyana and Rivien to follow her down the hall.

"I really think you should wait for Mr. Strong," protested the charge nurse, although it was not clear to whom she was addressing her plea. If it was to Nurse Pike, the senior nurse paid her no heed and continued to stride toward a small but comfortable family room at the end of the hall. The room was outfitted with puffy vinyl couches, more soothing art, and dim lighting from a Himalayan salt lamp in the corner. A coffee percolator chatted to itself quietly in the corner.

"With what may I help you?" asked Nurse Pike, who was exactly as Dr. Landry had described her. She had to be in her late seventies. She wore traditional nurses' whites, including opaque white pantyhose and nursing clogs. She had on her nursing cap, decidedly a more yellowed shade than her gown, which made Rivien wonder if it was the same cap as had been bestowed upon her at her nursing graduation. Her cross was indeed substantial, but Rivien had seen bigger, and it seemed to suit the stately woman in front of them. She held herself erect and moved quickly, efficiently, as she settled them into the family room.

Priyana turned to Rivien, signaling she was free to take the lead, and Rivien silently appreciated her trust while still wishing they had discussed their strategy beforehand. "Mrs. Pike, we're here investigating a formal complaint to the College about Dr. Josh Landry. We were hoping we could ask you about any information you might have in this case."

"Certainly. I will try to answer your questions appropriately, but please let me clarify something. You mentioned at the desk that you"—she nodded toward Priyana—"are from the College, but you"—she indicated Rivien—"are representing the medical examiner. What exactly is the nature of the complaint against Dr. Landry?"

Damn, this old broad is quick, thought Rivien. She liked her for it.

"Sorry, yes. I am trying to remain respectful of patient confidentiality," Rivien fibbed to cover her purposeful half-truth. "Two recent deaths in the facility have been flagged, stemming from the College complaint. That has prompted the ME's office to investigate, at least gather more information."

"I see. I am not sure if you can share the names, but I do think I know the patients to whom you are referring. It was quite unfortunate that one died in only Dr. Landry's presence, and the other, very shortly after he left. That being said, there is nothing suspicious I can think of in those situations. I have found Dr. Landry to be a very capable doctor, obviously one who cares very much for his patients. Having been nursing for well over forty years, there is not a death in this facility, or any other, that would shock me. People die every day, and I see no reason why two deaths in our hospice would raise any concern about Dr. Landry's care."

Priyana and Rivien glanced at each other, mentally passing the baton at that point. "So you didn't raise the concern yourself?" Priyana asked. "Bring it to site management?"

"Certainly not. There may be moral and ethical issues about which Dr. Landry and I differ. But the man is a skilled physician, and our patients are lucky to have his care. He has always treated me with respect, may I actually say deference, and I would not speak ill of the man behind his back. Any concern I might have with him I would bring directly to his attention, and I did not have any concerns about the instances to which you refer."

Priyana and Rivien sat studying the woman who seemed, quite genuinely, to have no ill will toward Dr. Landry, despite their mutually admitted difference of opinion.

"Do you have any idea if any other nurses had concerns about this situation?" Rivien looked at Priyana, as if to remind her that Gerald's letter had indicated that the concern had been raised initially by nursing staff.

"I am entirely confident the nurses were not the source of the complaint directly to the College or medical leadership, and I am unaware of any colleagues with a formal grievance that they would take to Mr. Strong. That being said, I do know that he was quite distressed when he learned that the deaths had occurred. He only found out when he made informal rounds a few days later and went to check on Mr. Baskins, who was a personal friend."

"We heard that you may have also been friends with the deceased. Or that you at least went to church together. And with Mr. Strong."

"Certainly I did know them, yes. Our church is quite close-knit, although I was not social with them outside of Mass and church events. Mr. Strong has been a member of our church since he arrived in Coulee Butte a few years back."

"It must be nice for you to be able to work as a nurse in a facility associated with your church," Rivien said. "Not everyone gets that opportunity."

"My aunties were both nursing Sisters, my mom a teacher in a boarding school with the church. Certainly I am proud to be able to serve God by serving his people."

"It must be challenging to work in hospice care. We are so grateful for those people who find that calling," said Priyana.

"We all serve differently, and for different reasons. I have worked all over, and in all different kinds of nursing. This is my calling now. To help people find peace."

"Thank you, Mrs. Pike, you've been most helpful. We will be seeing Mr. Strong as soon as he gets here."

"I hope this issue may be resolved quickly, as we were advised yesterday that Dr. Landry had been put on leave." With that, the stately nurse rose, smiled thinly but pleasantly, and exited the room.

"So," began Rivien quietly, "it doesn't seem to me that she is trying to hide anything. Josh may be right and they disagreed on some things, but I don't think she ratted him out. I mean, it wouldn't be very God-squad of her to lie to our faces."

"Agreed. She seemed genuine to me. I guess we will know more when we speak to Mr. Strong. We can ask him directly how he became aware of these concerns, as he stated in his letter that the nurses brought the complaint to him. And one of the victims was a personal friend? He failed to mention that in the letter."

"Do you think we should go wait for him at the desk?" asked Rivien.

"No, I don't think we'll have to. Pretty sure he will find us right quick when he gets here."

And with that, the two women helped themselves to coffee and waited.

CHAPTER 9

Mr. Gerald Strong was not happy to see them. "I am extremely disappointed you did not call ahead to set up a meeting with me as an initial follow-up to my complaint. Questioning my staff without me present is highly unethical. I thought you would show more professionalism."

Rivien, queen of the snap judgment, instantly disliked the man.

"You have initiated this visit through your complaint," said Priyana, "and I am sorry, but you do not get to dictate how the complaint is then investigated by the College."

For a tiny woman, Rivien thought, *Priyana is mighty.* Mr. Strong seemed appropriately chastised.

"Yes, all right. But I am in charge here. I thought you would want to talk to me first." Gerald was a short man, shorter than Rivien, and not quite as wide as he was tall. He was balding and wore a snappy suit and overly stylish glasses, which seemed a little out of place in Coulee Butte.

"We did," said Rivien. "You weren't here."

"What did Mrs. Pike tell you?" he asked, and Rivien decided to mark her territory too.

"We are not required to share information we have learned at this stage, sir," she replied, making up the rules as she went along but stating them with the bravado of the falsely confident.

Mr. Strong sat quietly, glaring at the two women, before he sighed, pulling his shirt sleeves out from his jacket cuffs. "Well, what can I help you with now?"

"We need to understand what prompted you to believe there was potentially something abnormal about the deaths of the two patients. What led you to become concerned, or even aware?" asked Priyana.

"Okay, I didn't feel like I could put this in the written complaint, not until I knew you were going to take it seriously. You are right, I don't hear about every death here, and I'll admit, it wasn't actually a nurse that tipped me off. I came up to the floor to look into it on my own."

"But why?" asked Rivien. "Did you have something against Dr. Landry?"

"Heavens no, I mean not personally or anything. But I have a colleague, a friend who is a pharmacist at the hospital; he told me there was suspicion of some…irregularities. I am sure you are aware that Dr. Landry is a MAID provider, and that all the MAID drugs are prepared and dispensed from the hospital pharmacy, at least in this community. Well, my friend said there was some concern that Dr. Landry might be diverting drugs. My friend does not dispense the MAID drugs; it is against our religion so he is a conscientious objector, but he has worked with a pharmacy technician to destroy the returned medications once they are no longer intended for the suicide."

"What made your friend 'concerned'?" Rivien asked, wondering how a "conscientious objector" would even know enough about MAID protocols to assess if anything was amiss.

"My friend said that one time, he and a colleague were disposing of some partially used MAID drug syringes, and they felt that one of the drugs, a white one, was not as opaque as it should have been. Excuse me, but I am not a clinician, so I can't recall the name. But it is apparently a solid white and the medication that was returned was more a cloudy clear liquid."

"But if your friend doesn't believe in MAID, how would he even know what happened at a provision, or how the medications were used?" Rivien asked.

"When my friend mentioned it, his tech said she had never noticed that before, and didn't know how to explain it. They consulted another pharmacist, who actually prepared the meds for MAID, and apparently she said there is no reason for that to happen. When it occurred another time, the three of them involved their manager, who agreed to send the most recently returned medications away for analysis. The rest of the drugs are clear anyway so there is really no way to know what the returned syringes actually contained without testing them."

"Why didn't you inform the College of this in your initial complaint?" asked Priyana.

"Because the test results aren't back yet, and my friend really should never have told me, as nothing has been confirmed so far."

Rivien knew that usually when a physician was misdirecting medications, especially benzos or narcotics, it was for personal use. Sadly, many physicians had lost their lives to this particular demon.

"So your friend decided to what? Give you the local gossip? Why? Was he trying to get Dr. Landry in trouble? Even if he was trying to get to the bottom of what was going on, no offense, but why come to you? This issue with the meds didn't even happen in your facility."

"That's the thing. My friend—his name is Michael, Michael Clubb—he told me because of the two deaths here. We were at the funeral for one of the patients, at our church, and I mentioned to Michael the circumstances of the death, that it was so sudden, even if not unexpected, and that only Dr. Landry had been with the patient at the time. Michael got really quiet, and I asked him what was going on. That's when he told me about the possible misdirected medications, the possible tampering. He wondered aloud, to me, if Dr. Landry could have been diverting them to use on other patients."

"I think it is premature to be making such accusations, don't you? You are basically accusing Dr. Landry of stealing from his legitimate MAID cases to commit actual euthanasia. Deciding for himself when people should die?" Rivien said incredulously. Although the initial complaint had certainly raised this possibility, to hear the accusation of murder put forward so bluntly was a shock. There are always complaints of poor medical care or judgment, even negligence, tossed around in social media and hospital hallways, but it was a big leap to active, premeditated murder.

Priyana calmly asked, "Did Dr. Landry know that he was under suspicion for tampering with the unused MAID medications?" Rivien wondered at her composure. She thought perhaps Priyana had firsthand experience with cases of doctors killing patients, like the cases Karen had mentioned that made the news during the pandemic.

"Not as far as I know. Again, the pharmacy department was not going to initiate a complaint without evidence. The initial belief was that he might be using the drugs himself, but they did not have evidence yet to approach the department head to request a toxicology screen on the doctor. The idea that the medications could be used a different way did not really dawn on anyone until the abnormal deaths here. I felt I needed to raise the alarm now so that no more medications could be potentially redirected while the lab testing was in progress."

"Okay," said Priyana, "I will need Mr. Clubb's contact information at the hospital pharmacy as well as the pharmacy manager's name so I can confirm where the testing is being done and when results may be expected. The College will not suspend a physician license without proof of wrongdoing but can closely monitor the situation and request practice supervision to ensure patient safety. I will need to speak to the pharmacists today."

As Gerald provided Priyana with the appropriate contact information, Rivien considered the white drug that Gerald had mentioned. She was barely aware of Priyana thanking Gerald for his time and handing him a card, ensuring him she would be back in touch with any further questions.

As the doors closed on the elevator, separating the two doctors from prying eyes and ears, they both spoke at the same time.

"He must mean propofol."

"So another church person is involved."

"Okay, okay. You go first, Priyana. I'm still floored. Actual murder."

"I know. I hoped it wasn't this, but I was worried. We don't know anything for sure, but even these kinds of accusations, they are so damning. For the doctor, for all of medicine."

"But a straight-up murderer. Have you ever dealt with a case like this?" asked Rivien.

"Myself, no. But sadly, I had a colleague who was involved in an investigation in India. A nurse who had murdered many people. She was targeting severely handicapped children and adults, thinking she was showing mercy. It was terrible, absolutely devastating. To the families, to the other workers who blamed themselves for not catching on sooner."

As she finished her story, the elevator doors opened on the main floor. As Rivien was about to open her mouth, Priyana put her finger to her lips and they hustled out of the building and down the steps. They headed directly to the car, and after they both hopped in and closed the doors, they continued the conversation as if there had never been a pause.

"When I was in school, I heard about a nurse in the US. He hurt patients and made them code, and then he would jump in to save them, which he sometimes did since he knew what had caused the code. But sometimes he didn't. They caught him fairly quickly, but still, how does someone like that become a nurse or doctor?" said Rivien.

"I know. And certainly Nurse Pike did not seem to see those qualities in Dr. Landry, and I am sure she has dealt with every possible type of doctor in her career."

"I bet," Rivien said. "So the drug, the one that Gerald was talking about, the white one, that has to be propofol. I didn't know that was in the protocol for MAID, but it makes sense. It's used in the OR every day to put people to sleep."

"I will take your word for it. I was a psychiatrist. Didn't do too much work in the OR."

"Crazy, I never even asked you what your speciality was before. Makes sense."

"I have heard that before but never know how to take it," said Priyana with a sly smile.

"No, no, it's because you actually seem to listen. Not all docs are good listeners, or seem to care about how people actually think."

"Yes, I remain fascinated to this day with how the human mind works. Like you said, how does someone believe themselves to be helping, when they are objectively, by all standards, doing harm. How do we balance the good, and the bad, that we do with each decision?"

"And how do we live with the good and the bad that we do? Oh boy, this is a mess."

"My other thought—and I'm sort of surprised it wasn't your first thought—was that now we have another church member involved in this mystery, Mr. Clubb," said Priyana.

"Yeah, so the two patients, Nurse Pike, Gerald, and this Michael guy all go to the same church. And then there is Dr. Landry, on the other side of this issue."

"Well, Nurse Pike did not seem bothered by Dr. Landry's actions, or beliefs, outside of the care he provided to the patient."

"Yeah, she seemed solid. But what about this Michael? If you are so against MAID you are not willing to mix up the meds, are you in an objective position to adjudicate the process?"

"But if the meds were tampered with, that is a very serious charge, and maybe it was even harder to come forward, knowing people might believe you had ulterior motives."

"I am glad you can see the gray, Priyana, because you aren't wrong. My natural skepticism definitely makes it hard for me to trust religion over science."

"But maybe for some people, they aren't mutually exclusive. It isn't choosing one over the other; maybe they can coexist."

"Like for Nurse Pike? Maybe. But whatever belief you hold, if you hold it so strongly that you are willing to apply it to other people, even against their wishes, then that is wrong. But maybe that is exactly what Dr. Landry did. Might not be religious belief, but belief nonetheless."

"Yes, fixed and firmly held beliefs can be a source of strength, and also great destruction," said Priyana quietly.

"Yes. Extremism, whatever the justification—I guess that is the real danger," Rivien said, her hand drifting to the scar the bullet wound left in her upper chest. "When I got shot, it was a twisted religion, a mistaken belief in hate and vengeance, that did this to me. I know, too, that I had many friends praying for me to recover, I mean really praying. They asked their god to save me, and they did it because their belief was pure."

"So what we do now, is that we listen. We don't have to believe with them, but we do need to understand. We have to be open. That is how we keep our minds flexible. That is how we respond," said Priyana, placing her arm around Rivien and giving her a little squeeze.

"Okay. Agreed. So what now? Do we go straight to the hospital pharmacy?" asked Rivien.

"Yes. We will interview who we can at the pharmacy before the end of their work day. Find out how the suspicions arose, and see when the testing results can be expected."

"Should I call Karen? I don't even know if they can test a body—the one that was buried—for propofol metabolites. Would they exhume them?"

"I really have no idea. So let's try to talk to the pharmacist first. If there is enough there for suspicion, I guess it doesn't hurt to ask Karen if that is even possible."

"Okay, I'll do that after the pharmacy, when I get a chance." As Rivien shoulder-checked and pulled away from the curb, she threw a little rearview mirror salute to a statue of the Virgin Mary that stood in the corner of the hospice lot, near a bench and another lush flower bed. *What must it be like to be you,* thought Rivien. *I certainly don't envy you, sister.*

CHAPTER 10

As Rivien drove through the small city, she pointed out her favorite parts to Priyana.

"This is the actual coulee that the town was named for. It cuts through the center of town, and the whole thing is filled with trails, playgrounds, ball diamonds."

"It is really lovely, like a prairie version of Central Park," Priyana said.

"Yeah. It is a nice city." Rivien was always happy to show people around. Coulee Butte held some of her best memories, and also some of her hardest. But in the early afternoon sun, she could very easily focus on the good. "I can drive almost anywhere in town in about ten minutes, which is great for kid pickups and activities."

"Is your daughter's preschool close to your home, then?"

"Pretty close. She's been at the daycare preschool near the hospital since she was two. I was working at the hospital and my clinic nearby when I picked the place. Before that she was in a dayhome."

"Have they been good places for her? I know my family struggled so much to find good care in Toronto. It's so expensive."

"They've been great."

"Is her dad around to help?"

"There is no dad in the picture. I decided to have her on my own. I was ready and hadn't met the right guy. I always wanted to be a mom, so I found a donor and now I have my little sweetheart. I feel like I won the lottery."

"That's amazing! It is lovely to have a partner, to have support, but only when it works out. I wish more women had the chance—or took the chance—to separate the desire for children from the desire for marriage. I was lucky in my marriage, and in my family, but I know many who were not."

"Agreed. I have a great family too. My mom helps a lot. My sister doesn't live here, but she is a great auntie as well."

"And no men in your life now? You'll have to excuse me, matchmaking is something of a hobby for me," Priyana said with a mischievous grin.

"I already have one Jewish yenta in my life, and if my mom hasn't succeeded in pairing me off, you've got your work cut out for you!" Rivien laughed. "Actually there is a guy, sort of. From last fall, up in Palladium City, the cop."

"Oh, excellent, a man in uniform."

"Except he's not here, he got reposted out east. He's a great guy, and Rita loves him, but I don't actually want them to get too close if this isn't a long-term thing."

"Oh my, that is so much for you to think about. I am glad I am older now, and my life is settled. My kids are close to your age, but you never stop worrying about your kids."

"Yes, I can vouch for that already," Rivien said as she turned toward the doctors' parking lot at the hospital before jerking her wheel to course correct into the public lot. "Sorry, habit."

"It's all right," said Priyana. "I was thinking that here, at the hospital, we had better ask to speak to the pharmacy manager. I am glad we launched the sneak attack on Mr. Strong, but I don't think that will fly here, and I don't want either of us to get a bad reputation in the hospital. So I think we should ask to speak to the pharmacy manager first and then speak to this Mr. Clubb."

"Okay," said Rivien as they strode toward the hospital and through the revolving door. "The pharmacy department is on the third floor. I am not totally sure who the manager is anymore, but we can ask when we get there. Let me pay for parking first."

"The College can pay," said Priyana.

"I'll send the ME the bill. Another advantage of a small town, cheap parking."

"Stop or you'll convince me to move here," said Priyana.

"And why not? Beautiful scenery, soon to be happening wine scene, only possibly murderous doctors."

Priyana's face went flat as she looked around to see if they had been overheard. But then she smiled. "You may not be working as a doctor anymore, but you haven't lost the morbid sense of humor, I see."

"Was the only perk of the job. Fucked-up sense of humor. You gotta laugh, or you'll cry."

CHAPTER 11

"Yes, I can confirm that Michael Clubb was the one, along with two others, who initially brought the possibility of medication tampering to my attention, as it related to the MAID provisions of Dr. Landry," said Anthony Hamish, the pharmacy manager. He seemed jittery to Rivien, but she couldn't quite tell if it was nerves, or if the man perhaps had a tremor, maybe even a tic. He was clearly trying to suppress it, so it was hard for her to delineate the etiology. He wasn't sweating, his gaze was steady, so she thought he might be dealing with his own medical issue.

Anthony continued, "MAID cases, especially those out of hospital where additional medications would be hard to come by urgently, are often sent with a large supply, not all of which are required in every case. The amounts administered to the patient are recorded and observed by a nurse at the provision, and any residual drug has to be returned to the pharmacy and accounted for."

"So was that not done correctly in Dr. Landry's cases?" Rivien asked, having no experience with providing MAID as a physician. The law had changed well after her residency, and her practice had not evolved to include this type of care.

"No, the paperwork had always been completed correctly, no flags had ever been raised. The tallies of the utilized and the returned dosages always equaled what was initially dispensed by our department. But returned meds are destroyed, their composition assumed as there is usually no reason not to, and no easy way to test their purity. The second time Michael came across the potentially diluted propofol and alerted me, it was sent away for analysis."

"Can we speak to Mr. Clubb as well, please," asked Priyana, and Anthony obliged by ringing his assistant and asking him to send Michael in to his office.

When Michael entered the room, Rivien saw he was an almost stereotypical nervous Nelly. Rivien had been a huge fan of the TV show *Scrubs*, having always found it by far the most accurate depiction of medical life, at least medical resident life, ever on screen. The character of Ted, the hospital lawyer, was known for his comical flop sweat and bumbling ineptitude. Rivien could not shake the image from her mind and had to bite her tongue to stop from laughing as Michael wiped sweat from his brow and bumped into a counter.

Priyana made the introductions and advised Michael that Anthony had already filled them in on the timeline of the initial concern being raised and the steps being taken to confirm or refute the suspicion.

"Mr. Clubb," Rivien said, "can you explain to me how a doc could possibly switch out drugs used in a MAID provision? A nurse is present for the whole provision and records the doses given. Never mind that, presumably, since patients are dying at these provisions, they have to be getting the good stuff, right?" The final line made Michael wince.

"I wondered that too," said Michael. "When I brought it to my colleague, the one who sometimes prepares the medications for an assisted death, to see if I was misunderstanding the situation, he said that when the doctor returns the drugs, they come alone. The nurse often stays behind with the family, waiting until the funeral home arrives."

"So the doc drives back to the hospital from wherever the death occurred with the med kit hanging out in their private car?" asked Rivien, thinking that it seemed a little haphazard. What if a cop pulled the doctor over on their way to the provision? *Are docs allowed to have large doses of narcotics in their own cars? Guess so.*

"Yes. When they arrive, the dispensing pharmacist and the doctor both initial that the doses used and the doses that remain equal the dosages initially dispensed."

"So how did you come to notice the returned medications looked different? You weren't involved in the signing back in of the remnants. You were only in charge of disposing of them, correct?" said Priyana.

"I only happened to look closely as I was ejecting the medications into the collection bin. That is a new practice, so we can recycle, not reuse, the plastic syringes. Before, the whole thing got thrown out together. Now we are trying to be more green, so I actually got to see the color of the propofol as it went in the receptacle. I don't think the doctor knows, I mean most don't, exactly how we dispose of medications here."

Michael looked down now, away from his boss and the two outside investigators. "I know I shouldn't have shared my concerns with Gerry, but I knew Dr. Landry worked at St. Michael's too. And I was worried. I wanted someone else to keep an eye on what was going on out there. I thought he would make sure Dr. Landry was acting like himself, you know, not depressed, or maybe overmedicated. I had no idea Gerry was worried that Dr. Landry was using the drugs on other patients until Gerry and I were talking at the funeral."

Priyana, and Rivien too, stiffened and looked at each other. Priyana covered, stating coldly, "We do not have evidence of that, and I do caution you to be very careful about who you share that information with. This department has made reasonable steps to investigate, and the College and the ME are involved now. There is absolutely no reason for this to become gossip, as that does not protect the public in any way." Anthony nodded his agreement and glared daggers at Michael. He certainly wouldn't want to expose the department to a defamation complaint if this all came to nothing.

"When do you expect the results of the analysis on the returned syringes?" Priyana asked.

"Obviously, it is not common practice for our department to have to send our own medications for testing; we aren't the medical examiner. So we actually had to dig into options, and I had to talk to the city to see if they had any experience with this type of thing," answered Anthony, stalling, his tremor more noticeable.

"And…" prompted Priyana, not about to be put off.

"It will still be a couple of weeks, maybe even another month. Now that you are here, maybe you could speed it up by calling the lab."

Priyana and Rivien got the lab's contact information, thanked Anthony and Michael, and headed back into the hall. When they walked past an empty patient room, Priyana waved Rivien inside and spoke quietly.

"We need to go back to Dr. Landry. There may be something here. He has only had his St. Michael's privileges suspended. They are free to do that if they want, but this hospital has not taken any action. I can't suspend his license—there is due process required for that—and we are not there yet. But I am obliged by law to take steps to ensure patient safety, even if just in the interim. We need to go talk to him. We can't tip him to the medication investigation yet, especially with those timelines, but we will need to arrange a chaperone for his practice in the short term."

"Yes. I want to see how he reacts when you tell him that. I don't suppose he'll be happy, but maybe he will give something away."

"Yes, we'll have to be alert," said Priyana.

"I need to go pick up Rita. Do you think we could meet up with Dr. Landry later, maybe five-ish? Rita has a friend who always wants a playdate, and I am sure her mom would let Rita stay for an hour or so if I could drop her off. I can go get her when we are done with Dr. Landry."

"Yes, I am sure that is fine. While you go for pickup, I'll call him, and will text you to confirm the plan."

"Okay, sounds good. I'll make sure Heather can take Rita for a little bit. I'll probably be about thirty minutes, getting her there and settled. If it's a go, I'll meet you at his office."

"Sounds good. Now get going, mama."

CHAPTER 12

"But, Mama, I don't want you to go. Can you play with me?"

"I will, honey, as soon as I am back. I have one more thing to do, and you can have fun with Heather and Macy until I am back."

The tears started to well in Rita's eyes and Rivien felt her heart ache.

"You promise, Mama?"

"Of course I do, Nugget. And I won't be long. Mama has to get this work done, but you know I'd rather be with you."

"Okay, I go play." Rita sniffed and went to join Macy on the living room floor. Rivien took a deep breath, but even as she exhaled she could already hear her daughter's laughter. The crisis had passed in her little world.

"Don't worry about her," said Heather, Macy's mom. "You know they are going to have a blast. I really appreciate you bringing her. It gives Macy something to do since she is stuck here with me all day."

"I know. And I'm really not busy many evenings now at all. But kids still know how to make you feel guilty, don't they?"

"I don't think they do it on purpose."

"No, of course not. I'm the one being dramatic now. I like to think I'm doing good, trying to model that Mama has other things on her plate, and that's okay." Rivien quickly thought her comment might be misconstrued as a slight against stay-at-home moms, so she rushed on. "I mean, you know, so that she gets used to it, for when I get busy at the store. Part of why I didn't want to be a doctor was to spend more time with her, so I feel guilty every time I pick work over her."

"You are not picking work over her, and trust me, she does know that. You need to work right now, and that's okay. Cut yourself some slack. She knows you're there for her, that is all that matters."

"Thanks, Heather, I really needed that today. I better get going, then. I'll get through this meeting and then hustle back. We'll be out of your hair before dinner."

"You know you're welcome anytime, and if something comes up, I'm happy to feed her too. Just let me know."

"Thanks. For everything," Rivien said, as she cast one last glance at the girls, who were serving each other fake ice creams and acting out crippling brain freezes. When she got in the car, she let her phone connect as she turned it on, and then dialed Karen as she pulled away from the curb.

"Hey, Rivien, how's it going?"

"Well, it's a bit more of a shitstorm than I hoped."

"Uh-oh, what's going on?"

"Well, there is some suspicion, no evidence yet, that Dr. Landry may have been misusing MAID medications from the hospital. Stealing some of the leftover drugs that had been supplied for legitimate cases, and returning the rest watered down."

"Oh no. So you found out about this while looking into the hospice deaths? Does that mean someone thinks he was using the stolen meds on the hospice patients?"

"I think that at least a couple of people have put two and two together and gotten five."

"So you don't think that is what's happening?" asked Karen. "I sure hope not."

"I can't know, nobody can right now. There are certainly a few people here who probably hope that is what's happening, might play into their beliefs in the evils of MAID."

"Any time a doctor gets accused of stuff like this, true or not, it is bad for everyone, and the public trust erodes even more, " Karen said.

"I hear you. That is why I'm calling. We need to get some evidence, at least something that might be more objective than gossip. Priyana—the associate registrar from the College—she and I are going to go see Dr. Landry again right away. I called you to see if it is possible to exhume a body and test it for propofol. Based on what I have heard, it is really unlikely the patient would have been getting that in hospice, but I can of course check their medication record to be sure. But if they weren't, if we could confirm propofol was in their system, that would be pretty damning."

"Yes, you are right. I mean it still doesn't prove how it got there, but it would certainly be enough to prompt a criminal investigation."

"So can you do it? I mean one body was cremated, right? So we only have one to work with?"

"Yes, one is already cremated. I believe that, yes, it is theoretically possible to test for metabolites of propofol, but I'd have to phone around to see what the options are. We don't have that specialized equipment in-house, so we would need to contract it out, possibly at an academic institution. There's cost associated with that, but for a possible killer-doctor, I am confident I can get it budgeted."

"I think we should do it. It will give us the answer."

"Whoa, whoa. I said it is possible, but these things are rarely simple. A positive answer would obviously be helpful, but a negative doesn't necessarily rule it out. There are so many factors in whether a sample can be processed or not. The time delay obviously being crucial, but often substances can be found for many years."

"Oh, shit," Rivien said, hitting the brakes.

"What?"

"Sorry, sorry, that wasn't about you. I made a shitty lane change. I'm distracted. But I still think we should do it, since it's only been a couple of weeks."

"But time is only one factor. I'll have to see if embalming was done. And then of course there's the issue of the initial dose. If these were stolen leftovers, and these patients were frail to start with, even if propofol was given, maybe only a small amount was needed. It would be harder to identify than a massive overdose."

"Why are you wet-blanketing my uneducated enthusiasm?" Rivien said with a laugh.

"Ha ha, because that is my job. Temperance. But I hear you. I will start looking into the options. I don't even want to think about asking for the permission to exhume yet. That will light all hell on fire, and I don't want to get to that step unless we know we are going forward. You keep digging with Dr. Landry and the investigation there, and I'll start looking into our testing options."

"Okay. I'll let Priyana know we talked, but I won't sell this as the smoking gun. Let's see how things go with Dr. Landry first."

"Agreed. And keep me posted. It sounds like you are having fun."

"Well, I wouldn't call it fun, exactly…" *Except maybe I would,* thought Rivien.

"I knew you were the right person for the job."

"Thanks, Karen, chat soon."

Am I having fun? This was about people's lives, and their death. How could it be "fun"? But it was also a mystery, a challenge. Rivien knew in her heart that Karen's assessment had been correct.

CHAPTER 13

The conversation with Josh Landry was going about as well as Rivien had expected.

"I am sorry," Priyana said. "But the College has a mandated responsibility to ensure patient safety, and we take that seriously, as it is the cost of self-regulation."

"Whatever happened to innocent until proven guilty?" Josh asked. He was pacing in the same waiting room where the investigators had met with him earlier in the day.

"No one is saying you're guilty," Priyana assured him. "We don't even know anything inappropriate has actually happened. This is really as much for your protection too. If there are people in this town casting aspersions, then a chaperone is your chance to have a third party verify nothing untoward is happening in your practice."

"The alternative is that the College believes me, just supports doctors rather than trying to kowtow to all the whiners. Nowadays it's totally acceptable for everyone to preach and protest about *their* rights, while trampling on the rights of anyone who thinks differently."

Rivien remained silent. The management of Dr. Landry and any potential risk he posed going forward was fully in the College's wheelhouse.

"I know you are frustrated," Priyana continued. "I really do understand. But this is not about supporting one ideology over another, it is about due process and regulation."

"Maybe I should quit, move somewhere else where they actually want me, where they aren't so backward."

"Please don't do that. Not complying with a College investigation or direction does not help you prove your innocence."

"So what am I supposed to do, then? I'm a family doc. I can't afford to hire a chaperone to watch me all day. In case you haven't realized, the kind of care I do is not the kind the government supports with big wads of cash."

"There have been no concerns raised about any other aspects of your care, nothing from your office. As such, as associate registrar, I am only going to stipulate a chaperone for palliative care consults and rounds, or MAID cases."

"They pulled my privileges at hospice already, it will only be my palliative consults at the hospital. But my MAID cases are mostly in people's homes. And I have one tomorrow, so how am I supposed to find a chaperone the College will accept before tomorrow? In case you haven't noticed, not everyone in the world agrees to be involved in MAID."

Rivien was momentarily distracted by her phone, having felt a buzz which a quick glance confirmed as a notification from Rita's preschool. As she briefly confirmed it was not something serious, just a field trip reminder for the next day, she had the feeling she was being watched. When she looked up, Priyana was looking at her intently, and Rivien saw Josh's gaze join hers.

"Rivien, I know this is not part of your ME investigator role, but you would be an excellent chaperone until a longer-term solution can be determined," Priyana said.

Rivien's initial look of suspicion when she had glanced up from her phone was now trending toward anger, her elevated brows now furrowing into a silent expression of *What the fuck?* But then she noticed Priyana's own expression and she was amazed again at the silent communication between them. Priyana wasn't pleading, she was prompting. Rivien could feel her willing her to understand that the opportunity could be an invaluable insight into what actually goes on when a doctor knowingly ends someone's life. Being there would be infinitely more useful to both of their investigations than simply reading about it.

Josh said, "If Dr. Gilrie agrees, I can accept that. I'd way rather have a doc than someone who has no idea what is going on. Who has never stuck their neck out for any challenging cases."

Rivien opened her mouth to speak, but Priyana interrupted. "Then it's settled, Rivien can be the chaperone at tomorrow's provision, and Dr. Landry, you and I can work out future options at a later date."

Fuck, thought Rivien, *why did I agree to this? Wait a minute, I didn't. Damn, Priyana is good, sneaky good.* As the women stood to leave, Rivien shot Priyana a glance that said as much. Priyana just smiled slightly and bounced her shoulders once. She knew.

Once they had left the building, Rivien thought about chastising Priyana for committing her without warning, but she knew that the moment had passed, and Priyana was right anyway. Instead she said, "That was hard. I feel bad for him, really. I know what it feels like, to be a bit of a medical pariah."

"I know he feels persecuted, that this is about religion, or about the morality of MAID, but I think he may be overly sensitive about that."

Rivien took a breath. "I hear you, but I also know that's easy to say when you aren't the target. I can't tell you how many people came to my office, and to my face said, 'I don't believe in abortion, but' as they asked me to end their or their kid's pregnancy. I literally saw ex-clients on the anti-choice picket lines. I mean, we do the work other people don't want to, and then get vilified for it."

"You're right, and I'm sorry. I didn't mean to minimize."

"I know. And even if some of Josh's pushback is about the religion stuff, I think more of it is about being a doctor. We don't like being questioned, never mind accused."

"I can vouch for that. And I respect the impact on his livelihood, his reputation."

"I hated when I saw the line between my job and my very identity getting blurred. I didn't want to be just 'a doctor.' But I know there are lots out there, consciously or not, that identify themselves solely as the job. They are doctors first."

"I know. Some doctors we are working with, sometimes on discipline, say that after over a dozen years of postsecondary education, years of sacrifice, when the job lets them down, isn't the dream they had long held it to be, that that is the biggest betrayal."

"I can't even argue that most docs aren't egotistical," Rivien said. "I think most are. We like the idea of being special, being right. It's a huge fall when you realize you aren't special at all, and every day feels like it was created to remind you of that."

"I am sure Dr. Landry is feeling that on this particular day. And that is why I wanted you to chaperone him tomorrow. I do think you can understand his position, and that is a strength, not a weakness. For both of you. We aren't trying to prove something one way or another at this point; we need to understand. And I think you are in the best position to do that."

"If you mean to understand that this career can be one of constant struggle, then yes, I think I got it," Rivien said sarcastically.

"I meant, smarty-pants, that understanding takes experience, empathy, and knowledge. You can turn your back on your past career, Rivien, but it doesn't mean you can turn your back on who, and what, you are."

CHAPTER 14

J osh and Rivien met the next morning at the hospital, about
an hour before the MAID provision was set to begin. They
pulled into the parking lot at the same time and walked into the
hospital together.

"So you've never been to a MAID provision before?" Josh
asked.

"No, it got legalized after I was done residency, so I was a bit
late to the party," Rivien replied.

"Seems like something you might have gotten involved with,
until you were attacked. Besides abortion, MAID is one of those
hot-button medical issues, and I find that people who truly support autonomy in one arena tend to support it in others as well."

"Yes, you're right. I did a few assessments for patients, but
never a provision. I felt like I was having a hard enough time
keeping up on the advances in family medicine. I didn't really
have the bandwidth to add another service."

"I hear that. I watched so many people die, in such a bad
way, in my training. And I was a paramedic before med school.
I knew I needed to help, if I could."

"I grew up on a farm, a ranch actually," Rivien said. "My dad always used to say he couldn't believe what we put people through at the end of their lives, the misery. We are kinder to animals when we put them down to end their suffering."

"Yeah, you wouldn't believe how many people tell me the same thing. They would never let an animal go on living in pain, or cooped up in a cage, like they feel they are."

"I really don't want to get in your way today," Rivien said as they stepped into the elevator together. "Like Priyana said, I'm here to make everything official, so that no one has to worry about retrospective judgment or complaints."

"I know. It's no biggie, really. I get observers fairly often. Mostly med students or nurse practitioners who are considering joining the MAID team."

Rivien and Priyana had agreed she needed to see both the medication pickup and return as part of her observation, although they did not spell that out for Josh. As much as Rivien was uncomfortable feeling like she was judging another doctor directly, she did think that by seeing the process firsthand she would be better positioned to explain to Karen any opportunity for lapses or deliberate diversion that may have occurred in the cases of interest.

"Priyana called me this morning," Josh said, "to ensure everything was a go. She told me I didn't have to explain your role, especially to other staff. It's enough that you are here."

"What about to the patient? Did she say how we should deal with that?"

"She said it was more of a gray area, but that it was appropriate to say you were an observer who was learning about MAID, which is true."

"Would you normally get consent for a learner?"

"Yes, but in this case, the patient can't really refuse, can they, so I'm not going to put the option to them." As he spoke, Josh became tense and reserved for the first time since they connected that morning. They had arrived at the hospital pharmacy door, and Josh pressed the intercom button and was buzzed into the back room.

The retrieval of the drugs at the hospital was straightforward and went exactly as the pharmacists had explained to Rivien and Priyana. None of the pharmacists who precipitated the complaint were involved in handing over the drugs. The new pharmacist was friendly, and he and Josh chatted as Rivien listened. The meds came already drawn up in syringes, labeled with tags not only listing their contents, but also stating that those contents consisted of a LETHAL DOSE. *No shit, Sherlock.*

Rivien was fascinated that the drugs were carried in a large plastic suitcase that would have been conspicuous even to those who did not know what the package contained.

"Isn't that a little, um, obvious?" Rivien asked as she and Josh walked out of the hospital together. "I mean, does it not draw attention to what you're doing?"

"I know. I tried moving the drugs to this little cloth roll I have, almost like a chef's knife roll, but the pharmacy got on my ass about infection prevention and control."

"But these drugs are going to a person who is going to die. I mean, I think infection is the least of their worries."

Josh smiled. "If you are waiting for me to explain the asinine reasoning of this lofty institution, you are going to die waiting."

"You're right. What was I thinking?" Rivien said, smiling too.

"Why don't you follow me to the patient's house in your car," Josh said, more a direction than a question.

"I don't want to get lost or lose you and hold up the provision. Why don't I hop in with you." She couldn't tell him that there were factions in the hospital that thought he was using his solo travel time to alter medications and spirit them away for his own use. As far as anyone knew, Josh was unaware of the suspicions raised at the hospital pharmacy; they were on the down-low until actual evidence came to light. He remained aware only of the hospice complaint.

"Sure, that's fine. We have to come back here anyway to return the unused meds, so I can bring you back to your car then."

"Sounds great."

Rivien liked Josh. From what she had seen, he seemed like a doc who genuinely cared about his patients, and who stepped up to provide a service that others had shirked. "You know, I really am keeping an open mind about all this, and I don't work for the College. You seem to me to be a good doc. At least you're not hawking an unregulated rapid weight loss scheme or prescribing unnecessary vitamin infusions for profit."

Josh laughed bitterly. "Probably I should have been, though, less aggro. I mean, don't you know that pumping vitamins through an IV line is the most 'natural' thing you can do? What a joke. Guess I'm the dummy who chose to help a patient leave this world on their own terms, with dignity."

"I'm sorry it's come to this" was all Rivien could think to say.

As they drove, Rivien was aware she was giving Josh the benefit of the doubt, and she thought that was okay. She had not been sent to investigate him specifically; that was Priyana's role. She was meant to be looking into anything out of the ordinary with two deaths in a local hospice. She was trying to understand his practice, see how assisted deaths, and possibly euthanasia, could be carried out.

As they parked in front of a nicely maintained 1960s bungalow on a heavily treed street near the historical center of the city, Rivien went to open the passenger door until Josh gently caught her forearm.

"This patient is dying of esophageal cancer. He's had several surgeries, radiation, chemo but now can't swallow anything, is in constant pain with brain metastases, and is starting to become confused, if not from the cancer than from the medications to control his pain and nausea. He doesn't want to live on a gastric feeding tube and knows the tumor will eventually invade a vessel and he will drown in his own blood. He doesn't want to spend his last days shuttling back and forth to the hospital for useless chemo treatments."

Rivien opened her mouth, planning to say "Understandable," but elected instead to shut it and nod. They got out of the car and Rivien followed Josh up the flower-lined path bisecting a fastidiously maintained lawn. As they entered the patient's home, they were greeted by a red-eyed family member, and the sounds of Garth Brooks's "The River" being sung by a man with a strong voice and a beautiful acoustic guitar. The house had more plants than Rivien had ever seen in one place, save the arboretum where she took Rita anytime they went to the city. Rita had a fascination with plants, choosing them over zoo animals every time. *Maybe she will be a botanist, or at least a better gardener than her mother.*

As Josh took his giant plastic briefcase to a small table at the back of the room, Rivien tried very hard to pull her eyes from the family, who were taking turns hugging their loved one, and instead focus on the medications, on the actions Josh took. It seemed so calm, no confusion. Rivien had attended many, many deaths in her career. Some were an absolute dumpster fire; there was no way to mince words. Patients suffering, calling out for family that wasn't there. Dying in pain, in fear, or slipping away but with no loved one to gaze upon as they closed their eyes one last time. She had seen families running to the bedside, and then finding they were too late for a last goodbye. Families whose last interaction had been bad, with angry words said, always thinking there would be time to repent.

The situation here was different. No one was happy, but peace had mixed with the grief and made a unique blend of acceptance, relief, and something she had not witnessed at many deaths: gratitude.

The family all went into the kitchen, gently guided by a MAID nurse named Helen, who had arrived before Josh and had initiated two IVs for the patient while preparing the family. Josh stayed to complete the final consent with the patient, Rivien observing. That done, he moved his medications to within easy reach of the IV line and then went to meet with the family, Rivien tagging along like a useless appendage. As Josh spoke to the family, one man went back into the room. Josh didn't stop his instructions, but the nurse looked his way and raised an eyebrow.

"That's his lawyer," said one of the sons, as the sounds of a gentle discussion filtered in from the other room. "The priest declined to come when he heard it was a MAID death. He gave last rites yesterday but wouldn't come today. Bastard. Dad's lawyer used to be a part of the church too, but he's like us—not very religious anymore. But he said if the priest wouldn't come, he would at least, to be with him, say a prayer."

Rivien hazarded a guess as to why the majority of the family had turned their back on the all-too-frequent hypocrisy of organized religion. Yet their dad was here now, still with faith and yet breaking with his church's doctrine. *Nothing is black and white.*

As Josh finished his final discussion, the group returned to the patient's side and the nurse ensured the IV line was running well and all paperwork had been completed. Josh did not rush. He stood by as tears fell in the room like rain, peppered with an occasional rumbling thunder of laughter and jokes. It was surreal. It was a symphony of a full life, not just of an impending death. It was magical.

The patient, struggling to speak with his ravaged throat, rasped, "Let's get on with it, then."

Josh started the medications. They were administered in an IV by slow manual push, Josh controlling the flow by how hard and how quickly he depressed the syringe plunger. He quietly read the names of the drugs and the doses out to the nurse, who was recording them off to the side. Two medications—a benzodiazepine and a narcotic—had been given when Rivien first started to notice glances between Josh and the nurse.

Having never seen a provision before, Rivien was slower to react until she realized that the frail man had apparently been given a large dose of midazolam and fentanyl and yet remained alert and conversing with his family. Josh waited about a minute, then picked up the propofol, but after glancing very intently at Helen, he went back into his box of meds. He set the propofol down again and gave the remaining dose, all that remained in the syringe of the midazolam, calling this quietly out to Helen while acting like this was his plan. He looked up at the IV, checking it was running well, telltale drips falling steadily in the chamber.

There was no discussion between the two professionals. Rivien could sense something was strange to them, but she had no frame of reference. Perhaps this infirm man had become highly tolerant to drugs he had been receiving to suppress his suffering. No matter the cause, no one wants to hear, in the middle of any medical procedure, "Well, this isn't how we expected this to go." But Rivien could pick up that the team was surprised by the delayed or diminished reaction to the drugs, if not yet actually concerned. Rivien suspected every patient was different in assisted death, as they were in life, and maybe this was unusual, but not unheard of.

Josh then picked up the propofol syringe. As he held it aloft, Rivien carefully scrutinized its opacity, same as she had done when it was being dispensed at the pharmacy. It was a creamy white, and no light shone through it as Josh moved toward the IV. This syringe was larger, and there were two more of the same available in the suitcase. Josh was halfway through the first syringe when Rivien could see his eyes widen in first confusion, then alarm. Nothing much seemed to be happening with the propofol, a drug which tended to knock people out before they counted back from ten as far as six. But then something did happen, and it wasn't good.

The patient started to hyperventilate, and to shake and squirm in his chair. He was muttering, "Is this normal? Is this normal?" over and over. Some family members pushed closer to his side, others recoiled. Josh pushed in the other full syringe of propofol, hoping it would kick in, but it did nothing and the patient's distress increased rapidly.

The patient started panting, his face red and pinched, and then he convulsed, shaking wildly, his bladder releasing and his color rapidly turning to gray. His wife was crying loudly, and a son was yelling, asking what the hell was going on. Rivien stumbled backward, farther from the furor, as Helen pressed forward to check the arm with the IV, to make sure the IV was in place and running into the vein and not the skin. Josh was focused on his patient, clearly forgetting that Rivien was even present. He pulled out a stethoscope as the man slumped forward but continued to shake.

Rivien asked, "What can I do?"

"Check a pulse!" Josh blurted out, and when Rivien reached for the man's wrist, she could not even count the rapid rate, it was so fast. She looked back to instinctively check Josh's bag for resuscitation equipment and then retracted her hand, remembering this death was never intended to be reversed and that even in the chaos, there was only one outcome toward which everyone was striving, a peaceful death that was slipping away. As she stood, feeling completely useless, the patient gasped, shrieked, and then went limp. A second son knocked Rivien over from her crouched position as he rushed to his dad's side, shaking him to try to rouse him. Josh pulled his scope away from the patient's chest to lift Rivien to her feet. The nurse was rummaging in her bag, but there were minimal supplies here. The stethoscope was on its own.

"Is he dead?" screamed the patient's wife, and Rivien too looked at Josh, who had resumed his auscultation at the chest. He slowly shook his head and said something Rivien had not expected. "No, he still has a heartbeat. He is taking some breaths." As if on cue, the patient grunted, an agonal breath, followed by two more, then went limp again. His wife screamed.

"What the fuck happened?" came the response from the family, in a round.

"I don't know," replied a visibly shaken Josh, too stunned to even fake the confidence that so many physicians put on daily. "I don't know. This has never happened, it's like he didn't respond to the drugs at all. I think he got tachycardic, fast heart rate, maybe high blood pressure. I'm worried he may have had a stroke, or a heart attack."

"So fucking help him!" said his oldest son, getting right into Josh's face.

"I can't resuscitate him. He—that's not what he wanted, and I-I have no equipment anyway. I don't have any different medications here, no more sedatives, he didn't respond to what I used. He may pass quickly or..."

"Or what?"

"He may not, he may hold on, if his heart can keep pumping. I...I can't just give him the paralytic. I don't know what he can feel right now, I have no idea why the propofol didn't work. I could give some more, but it didn't work like it should. I don't think I can give him the paralytic." As if to confirm this, the patient flung back his head, moaned, and then flopped again to the side as his wife gasped again. "I think we need to call an ambulance, get him to hospital. He can be sedated there. Until he passes."

"You mean he could stay like this? Is he suffering? Can he hear me?" asked the wife, shaking uncontrollably, finally collapsing to the floor, caught before impact by one of her sons.

"I am so sorry, I don't know what happened. Let's get him to hospital, and we will try to figure this out. We can make him more comfortable there. I'll call right away."

"You do that, but then you get the fuck out of this house" came the response from the eldest son. "You fucked this up, he's worse off than he was. He could be stuck like this now. He could be in pain. Get the fuck out of this house right now. Call the ambulance but get the hell out. We want a different doctor at the hospital. Get out!"

Rivien was stunned. She had never seen anything like this. Helen was crying, and as Josh grasped for his supplies, he kept opening his mouth to speak and then closing it before anything came out. He finally grabbed the syringe case and his phone and went to the door. He shoved the syringe case at Rivien as he started dialing 911. As they stepped onto the porch, he requested the ambulance after answering the dispatcher's litany of questions.

Without speaking to Rivien or the nurse, he made a second call to the emergency department and relayed the issue to the on-service doctor. He had gathered himself enough that Rivien could follow his side of the handover.

"The meds didn't work. I don't know what was wrong with them. It's like he didn't respond at all and then responded the exact opposite as expected for propofol. I think he had a stroke." Silence again as the doctor on the other end of the line asked a question. "Yes, and get the on-call palliative care physician paged urgently to meet the ambulance in the ED, to get the patient comfortable as soon as possible. I'll ask the ambulance to give whatever they can for sedation, ketamine or morphine or something." He hung up. Helen was squatting beside her car with her head in her hands, crying.

Rivien and Josh stood on the porch and he turned to her now. "I don't know what the fuck happened, I've never seen this. I can't believe this happened. Oh, fuck. What the hell did I do? What the hell went wrong?"

"I don't know, I don't know," Rivien said, much louder than she had planned. "Let's go, let's get in the car. We won't leave, we can wait until the ambulance gets here so you can hand over, but we can't do anything more for them on their porch." Rivien could hear crying, wailing really, and raised voices from behind the sturdy door. It was unnerving, and she wanted to move away, to distance herself. "Let's look at the meds. Let's talk to the pharmacy. I don't know."

Josh started moving to the car but didn't say another word to Rivien. After the ambulance came and went, they drove back to the hospital in silence. Rivien had tried asking him if she should drive, where he wanted to go first, what they should do. She asked him if he wanted to call their medical malpractice insurance provider, ask for advice, which was standard protocol with doctors after a negative outcome. He never responded; he never even acknowledged her questions with anything more than an exhalation. She could see the entire scene being replayed behind his eyes, but she could not read the conclusions he was reaching. She was getting very uncomfortable by the time they pulled up in the emergency short-term parking at the hospital.

As Rivien stepped from the vehicle, she said shakily, "I think we should go to the pharmacy first and—" but before she could complete her thought, Josh accelerated away from the curb. She lost her grip on the car door as it was yanked from her, and she fell forward onto the sidewalk as he squealed away, the passenger door snapping shut as he made a hard turn out of the parking lot. A security guard ran to Rivien's aid, but she was unhurt, only confused. Despite her lack of physical injury and against all her will, she began to cry. The security guard looked at her suspiciously, seemingly not having recognized her, or Josh, and likely questioning if this was a lover's spat or one of the more serious domestics that found their way to the facility. She waved off the guard's vain attempts at comfort or assistance and assured him, through stifled sobs, that she was okay.

She plopped down on the curb in front of the hospital. Overwhelmed, she was not even concerned, as she normally would be, about potential embarrassment if former colleagues walked by. *What the fuck is Josh doing*? He had to address this. He needed to hand over to the palliative doc and to figure out what the hell happened with the drugs. *The drugs!* They were still in Josh's car. And now they were gone.

Rivien knew she needed to track Josh down, speak to him as soon as possible. She tried to call him, but it took three tries to even get her phone to unlock, her facial recognition apparently struggling with her already puffy eyes and blotchy complexion. She called his number but got no answer. She wasn't sure where he lived or where he might go. She had so many questions she needed to ask him.

It would turn out she would never get the chance.

CHAPTER 15

J osh was found that night.

Rita was snuggled up in her own bed. Rivien had read her a story, as was their nightly custom, and then busied herself around the apartment with dishes, laundry, and packing lunch for tomorrow's preschool day. But even as Rivien lay in her bed, listening to the dulcet tones of her child's snores on the monitor, she could not pause her mind. She eventually admitted defeat and moved from her bed to the couch, where she fell asleep to the mundane chatter of her TV until she was startled awake by her phone.

"Hello," she said, still able to spring to life in the middle of the night, the product of many conditioning years on call.

"Rivien, it's Priyana. I'm sorry to wake you, but I thought you'd want to know."

Rivien had called Priyana after Josh had sped away, replaying the horrific incident at the patient's house, and Josh's disappearing act. The two women had planned to meet for breakfast in the morning and then look for Josh, once he'd had a chance to decompress.

"What is it? What's going on?"

"It's Josh. He's dead. I got a call from Gerald. He still had my card."

"What? Dead? How? He only left me earlier today!"

"Suicide. That's what Gerald said. They found him in his car, in his garage. It appears to be carbon monoxide poisoning. The car was still running when the police got there."

"Oh my god. I can't believe this. I mean, I know he was upset—who wouldn't be?—but that can't be the first time something shitty has happened to him with a patient. What a mess. I'm so sorry, so sorry he did that."

"I know. I feel so guilty. We talked to him and then right afterward he had that terrible case and now this. He must have felt so trapped, so alone. I'm kicking myself. I can't stop wondering if we could have done something differently."

"I shouldn't have let him go," Rivien said. "I should have talked to him more about it, tried to debrief, but I couldn't stop him."

"I know," said Priyana. "I'll call the registrar in the morning. Gerald said he gave the police my info too, so I could fill them in on what Josh's mindset might have been when he did this."

"Really? Why couldn't Gerald tell them himself? You can't release confidential information."

"Yes," Priyana said, "I found it strange too. And although I am glad to know, I am not sure why he felt he needed to call me in the middle of the night."

"Likely trying to pass the buck. Make us feel bad, like it was our investigation that caused this, even though Gerald was the one who initiated the complaint. And how did he even find out so fast? It's not like he was next of kin."

"You're right, I think he is trying to save face. He told me he was the one that called in a wellness check on Josh. Even though he had concerns, Gerald claims he still greatly respected

Josh and knew he was very stressed and going through a lot. He said he tried to call Josh to talk this evening, and when he got no response after multiple attempts, he called the police to do a check on him. That's when they found him."

"Going through a lot? He wouldn't be going through anything if that busybody hadn't gotten all worked up about his church friend's death. And he knew everything Josh was going through well before tonight. He pulled his privileges before today..." Rivien trailed off into thought. "Fucking bastard!" she murmured as a thought crystallized in her mind.

"Excuse me?" said Priyana, slightly more proper and less prone to casual profanity than her younger counterpart.

"Gerald must have found out about the MAID case going wrong. That's the only thing that changed in the last twenty-four hours."

"But how could he have found out?"

"That fucking pharmacist. Michael. When Josh took off, he took the drugs with him. The pharmacy was waiting not only to sign them in, but to send them for testing, like the others, to ensure they were undoctored. I called up there. I didn't speak to Michael, but I did reach the head pharmacist. I didn't give any details, I swear, but I did say there had been an issue. I said the leftover drugs couldn't be returned yet, and that I would update him. There really wasn't a lot left, since Josh had tried everything when the patient had complications. So that's why I wasn't concerned with him taking them; there was hardly anything left. But they needed them signed back in for MAID accounting."

"So you think Michael found out something went wrong and called Gerald? Would that be enough to raise Gerald's suspicions about Josh's mental state?"

"I don't know. Those two assholes are sharing information, even when they have no right to. I get the feeling Michael likes to feel important, especially to Gerald. I wonder if he's trying to suck up to some big shot at the church?"

"I don't know, but you're right, it was inappropriate. But it doesn't really change that Gerald was right; Josh was not well, not doing well at all. How sad. I mean, there's a good chance he did nothing wrong, nothing other than make a clinical mistake, maybe."

"Agreed," said Rivien. "We have no evidence he ever set out to hurt people, or to do anything he shouldn't, but now that he's gone, some people are going to believe that is an admission of guilt."

"That's true," said Priyana. "Gerald said, 'I guess he couldn't live with what he'd done' or something like that. As much as he doesn't want the blame…"

"He's also trying to take credit for stopping a 'bad man,' " Rivien said, finishing Priyana's sentence. "Self-righteous bastards."

"You know," she continued, "I was with Josh the entire time today. I literally did not leave him alone with the drugs for a second. I drove with him and everything."

"Yes, you told me that."

"So I know Josh did not tamper with the meds. He couldn't have. And yet, these ones didn't work, something went wrong. They came directly from the pharmacy to Josh."

"Maybe it was something about the patient, something metabolic, or a cross-reaction with another medication he was on, an adverse event?"

"Maybe. Or maybe Josh was given the wrong drugs. Maybe someone at the pharmacy tampered with them?"

"You don't think Michael would do that, do you? Not after he raised suspicion about Josh in the first place. Wouldn't that be too obvious?"

"I guess so. And supposedly he isn't around any of the MAID drugs when they are prepared, anyway. It would be strange if he suddenly inserted himself," Rivien said. "I feel like there is something else going on here, we just haven't seen it yet."

The two women stayed on the phone in silence, but with a mutual understanding that any establishment of guilt in this situation was not yet done and dusted.

"So what now?" asked Rivien. "Do I keep investigating? Do you? I guess I'll call Karen."

"Yes. You should call her in the morning, but I think she will say to stay on the case, still do your report. Because you were not investigating Josh, you were following up on unexplained or questioned deaths, which is the purview of the ME. For me, I have no regulated College member to investigate anymore. But I will still need to report to the registrar on this situation. I'm not leaving yet."

"So we can still work on this together?" Rivien asked, hopeful she would not immediately lose Priyana's level-headed presence.

"For now. At least I can take an unofficial back seat. You take the lead, but I want to know what happened here. This doctor didn't need to die, no matter what he felt or what others believed about him. He was not yet proven guilty, and if my being here in any way contributed to his death, the least I can do is learn from it and prevent a similar tragedy in the future."

Rivien was quiet, feeling again she was being called to speak for those who could no longer advocate for themselves. But she didn't know whose voice she was being summoned to become. Josh? The dead patients? All she knew was that the system had once again twisted the intentions, dreams, and aspirations of all those involved into a convoluted nightmare of failure.

CHAPTER 16

Rivien couldn't sleep. Her mind was still racing over her last interaction with Josh. She decided to call Justin, hoping the cross-country time difference and unpredictable cop hours might allow them to connect.

Hi, you've reached Justin's voice mail. Leave a message.

Rivien hung up and sent a text as follow-up.

Hey, you up? I could use a chat.

Minutes went by and nothing. Maybe he's sleeping, hopefully he is, maybe he's out doing something—or someone—else. *Stop it! You're the one who told him you couldn't commit, he has always been great, he'll text you back when he's up. Don't be dramatic.*

But Rivien still couldn't sleep. She sat on her couch, staring at a favorite piece of art. It was a scene from the badlands near her childhood home, a landscape Rivien had loved since childhood and which had lost no majesty for her in the intervening years. The canvas was large, over five feet wide, and framed simply in a thin black shadow-box frame. The panorama depicted the coulee hills along the river as the sun was setting and throwing shadow across the already undulating and mysterious hoodoos, magnificent in their permanence and inimitable beauty. The layered sedimentary stripes of muted color were intensified by the purple cast of the dusk and electrified by the blazing orange rays of the receding sun.

Fuck it, thought Rivien. *I'm calling her, she's probably up anyway.*

As her sister's groggy voice came on the line, Rivien knew she was wrong. "Riv, what the fuck time is it? Is everything all right? Rita?"

"Yes, sorry, everything is fine. I mean, not fine, but we're fine."

A pause. "So why the hell are you calling me at four in the morning?"

"I needed to talk to someone, and I was looking at your painting, and I thought you might be up."

"What? My painting? What are you talking about. I gotta work tomorrow."

"I know, I know. It's just, something bad happened, and I couldn't get hold of Justin, and...I don't want to talk to anyone other than you."

"I miss how we used to fight when we were kids. Back then you would have known better than to bug me," Edi said, but with no malice in her voice.

"Too bad it's not like before Rita was born, when you were off being a wild child. I probably couldn't have even found you and you'd have probably lost your phone anyway."

"Well, I'm a responsible lawyer now. So either start talking or start paying, I don't wake up at four except for the most well-funded drug dealers. Seriously, what is going on?"

"So a couple of days ago, I got asked to do a little medical examiner work, for that friend of mine who is an ME, from last summer."

"Riv, what happened to no more medicine?"

"Listen, Mom already gave me her 'I don't understand what you are doing with your life' spiel, but the nice version. God only knows what Dad thinks."

"Cool the pity party. Isn't that what *you* said? No more medicine."

"Yeah, okay, fine. I could use the money and this isn't medicine. I get to be a fake cop again. I am looking into some in-hospital, or hospice, deaths, gathering some info for Karen. That's it. The College is here, checking out the doc at the center of it, but my job is simple."

"It's four in the morning and you still haven't explained anything, so it can't be that simple."

"Yeah, well. The doc that was under suspicion about the deaths, he committed suicide tonight."

"Oh no, that's terrible!"

"Yeah, and it was after this horrible MAID case. I was there as an observer. The guy was having convulsions and—"

"Whoa, you know I don't want any blood and guts. I hate that shit."

"Yeah, I'm aware of your squeamishness, you baby. But really, Edi, it was bad. And the family was all there. It was a mess."

"So is that why he killed himself? I mean, it was nothing to do with you, Riv."

"I know, but maybe the investigation tipped him over the edge. But it was still so sudden."

"I don't think you need to be told that you never know what is in someone's mind. But either way—and playing devil's advocate here—"

"I'd expect nothing less."

"Smart-ass. You called me, remember? Anyway, how sure are you, or the cops or whoever, that it was suicide? Were there witnesses?"

"No, he was found in his car in his garage with the car running. That's pretty clear-cut, isn't it?"

"What I am gently trying to say is, despite your new little gig, you are not in fact a cop. So maybe get some more info, if you can. And no matter what, don't blame yourself. You can't control other people."

"That feels like a dig."

"I'm simply saying I know you like to help, and I know you get deep into things pretty quick."

"Quickly."

"Thanks, Mom. Jeez, you really are turning into her."

"Fuck off."

"Remember why you left medicine. Don't get sucked into other people's problems again. This isn't on you, and even if you are helping, it is not all your responsibility. Just do what you can and then walk away."

Rivien was quiet.

"It was hard, Riv, never forget that. Not just for you, but for us. Watching you get hurt, thinking we could lose you. Don't get sucked in again. That's your modus operandi."

"Yeah, I know. It's hard to turn off. I feel like there is something else going on here, something more."

"And I know it will kill you to let it be, but let it be. Do your diligence then put it to bed. Please."

"All right. I hear you. I'll let you get back to sleep now."

"Doubt that is going to happen."

"Well, thanks anyway, really. I needed to hear that tonight."

"Night, sis, love you."

"Love you too. Hey, can I ask you one more thing?" Rivien said, gazing again at the painting.

"Yeah" said Edi, somewhat suspiciously.

"Why did you never become a professional artist? You could have, if you wanted. Made a living selling paintings."

"Oh, please, you and Mom are basically the only people who like my art."

"That's not true and you know it."

Edi was silent for a moment. "Probably the same as you, why you became a doctor and why I eventually got my shit together to be a lawyer. We're practical people, Riv, practical people who wish they could be passionate and creative instead. It's a tug-of-war. Sure, I would have liked it, being an artist, some of the time. But I also like nice clothes and fancy holidays. But I'm proud of you, Riv, and I hope the store will be your passion—besides Rita, of course. Practicality isn't always what it is cracked up to be."

"I love you, sis."

"Love you too. Now don't wait until the middle of the night to let me know about your next crazy work plan. I can't take it."

"Deal."

"Night."

"Morning."

As Rivien hung up, she looked at her phone and realized she'd missed a call from Justin; she hadn't even registered the call waiting. She could see he hadn't left a message, and no text. *Tomorrow,* she thought. *Tomorrow.* Then she got up to brew coffee and to kill time for a few hours as she waited for the sound of tiny feet stomping madly to the bathroom.

CHAPTER 17

"Mama, I have a question" came the tiny voice from the back seat.

"Yes, Nugget, what is it?"

"Can I eat this?"

"Eat what? What are you eating?"

"I found it."

"Found what?" Rivien strained to see Rita in the rearview mirror before risking a glimpse to the booster in the middle back seat.

"This."

"What is *this*? Describe it. And don't eat stuff you found anyway."

"Aw, Mama, it's just a sucker."

As Rivien stopped at a four-way, she took the opportunity to turn to her child and came face to face with the proffered sucker, complete with attached tissue, adherent lint, and a tag-along errant Cheerio.

"Rita, don't eat that. Give it to me."

"But Mama."

"Give it."

"But what I am going to have for dessert?"

"Child, it is eight in the morning, you don't need dessert."

"But I finished all my breakfast."

"Breakfast doesn't have dessert. I put a treat in your lunch, you can eat it at snack time. We're here."

"Okay, Mama." Rita dejectedly slid from her booster seat, having learned how to release the buckle herself, and quietly exited the car through the door Rivien had opened. She perked up immediately upon seeing a friend climbing the preschool stairs, and the two besties chatted the rest of the way in, dumping coats and backpacks in the hall before being chastised by their respective mothers to put them where they belonged.

Rivien managed to catch Rita for a quick cheek smooch before she was off and playing again, drawn by the siren song of the water table, the greatest station in all preschool history. Rivien returned to her car, pulled away from the curb, but then parked again a block up, feeling she had done the fair thing by leaving space for more drop-off parents, but unable to wait any longer before calling Karen.

Rivien launched right in, as soon as her friend said hello. "I'm not sure if you got called last night, but the doc for the two cases you sent me to look into died last night—suicide."

"I actually did hear from my night investigator, right before you called. It's terrible, a tragedy for the doctor, his family, the whole community, really. But of course, I can't say it's suicide, not yet. I try really hard not to be swayed by the first impressions of the responders."

"I hear you," said Rivien, feeling appropriately chastised for her premature diagnostic closure. "Then let's say possible suicide. But Christ, what a mess this is now. Do you still want me fishing around, or is it in bad taste?"

"No," said Karen. "I need you now more than ever. I'm getting the doctor's body brought here ASAP, and I am going to start his autopsy today."

"Did anyone give you any information that might help me try to figure out what happened to the patients? Did he leave a note? Confession? I heard he was in his car."

"Yeah, in the garage," Karen said, "so suspect carbon monoxide poisoning. And no note. There was an empty bottle of pills on the floor of the car. Tricyclic antidepressants, based on the label. Not in his name, in a patient's. Unfortunately, my investigator already confirmed it was a patient at St. Mike's hospice, and the pills were missing from the patient's personal effects. This is all off the record right now. I know I can trust you, but this is captured by investigator confidentiality too, even though this wasn't your original case."

"Of course, without saying. But frick. A doc would know good meds to pick for a suicide. Couple that with the carbon monoxide and he wasn't leaving anything to chance."

"I'll run a full tox on his blood to confirm they were in his system."

"Wait a minute. When did he take the meds from St. Mike's? He did not seem suicidal—and yes, I do know that isn't always obvious—when we first met him. I sort of assumed the bad MAID case pushed him over, but when did he grab the meds? It had to be before he was suspended from the site. So had he been stealing for a while? Stockpiling for a suicide, or was he just taking whatever he could get his hands on for personal use?"

"But it's not like it's benzos or narcotics. Not too many people take TCAs for fun. And what bad MAID case?" Karen asked.

"Shit, did you not hear about that yet? Christ, is that patient still alive?"

"What patient?"

"On the day of his death, Josh had a terrible MAID case that I was unlucky enough to observe. It was horrific. The patient didn't die; he seized, maybe stroked, probably aspirated, and the family was all there. It was awful."

"No, I haven't gotten that report yet. So either the patient isn't dead yet, or the paperwork is in my basket and got bumped by Dr. Landry's death. That certainly could have contributed to his death. He was already worried because his cases were being investigated, and the College was there."

"I know. I feel sort of responsible."

"You're not, Rivien, and you know that. You are not responsible for someone else's actions."

"I know, but I feel I need to get to the bottom of this. He deserves that."

"Agreed. You're contracted to us now, so I can call you as soon as I know anything from the autopsy, and I'll keep my eyes out for a failed MAID death from your area too. I'll keep you posted on my end."

"Same here," said Rivien, but just as she was about to end the call, she blurted out, "What about the meds, the MAID medications, the leftovers. Josh took them with him after the bad case, didn't sign them back in. Did the police find them?"

"I don't recall anything like that in the report. I'll ask my investigator, and she can check with the cops, but the only medication listed was that empty bottle of TCAs."

"Where could they have gone? Did he get rid of them, like they were evidence? Or did somebody take them?"

The two women were silent. The location of the missing meds had not been considered until now.

"I will get my investigator to speak to the police," Karen said, "and if they haven't been found I will ask them to scour his house, car, or dumpster for them. I'll let you know. And one other thing, Rivien: this is interesting but it doesn't prove anything."

"Yes?" Rivien said, knowing already that *interesting* was doctor-speak for *fucked-up.*

"He was in the back seat. Josh," Karen said.

"What? Isn't that odd? How could he have started the car? Isn't that suspicious?"

"Yes and no. Actually about forty percent of carbon monoxide deaths in cars are in the back seat. It generally rules out it being accidental, but lots of suicides seem to want to, um, get comfortable."

"Shit, I never thought of that. It's not what you see on TV, right?" Rivien said, feeling stupid bringing it up, since almost nothing you saw on TV had any basis in medical fact. *Fact and experience don't matter! Give us drama!*

"All right," said Rivien, "I'll let you know what I find out on my end." As she disconnected, she knew who she needed to talk to next. As she hit Justin's contact picture to initiate the call, she ensured her hands-free was connected and pulled away from the curb. How was she going to explain to Justin that she had somehow found herself in the middle of another mess, like last fall? He was going to think she was cursed. Maybe she was.

CHAPTER 18

"Hey!" came Justin's cheerful opening, indicating to Rivien he was on a day off and not surrounded by coworkers. "Been a little while. How are you? How's Rita?"

"She's good. Obsessed currently with dragons. But it beats the unicorn phase so I'm good with it."

"And you? I miss you."

"I miss you too. I'm good. Well, I mean, I'm good, but something has come up."

"I'd ask if you were breaking up with me, but we're not really together. So I hope that isn't it."

"It's not." Rivien thought she sensed frustration in Justin's voice, but maybe that was her imagination. "So you remember Dr. Pinder, from last year."

"Yeah, what about her?"

"She moved to Alberta, and she's an ME here now. And she asked for my help on a case."

"I thought you were done with that, Riv. I want to hear more riveting info about grape varietals, and less about bodies."

"You're a cop. You're supposed to like dead bodies, aren't you?"

"No, I don't like them. I get paid to deal with them."

"Now I do too. It's a contract gig, a bit of extra cash."

"It's not like I'm going to talk you out of it, because you're probably already doing it, aren't you?"

"Yes. But once again, I bit off more than I can chew. It was supposed to be a brief contract to look into some hospice deaths, but the doc who was under suspicion of potential wrongdoing just died. It looks like a suicide."

"Looks like or was?"

"I don't know. Karen said the same thing. But it's a mess regardless."

"So, no offense, but are the actual cops involved now?"

"Yes, and none taken. Despite what you know of me, I really don't think I'm a cop, or want to be a cop."

"So are you done with this now?"

"Well…"

"Riv? Tell me you are done now. Give Karen what you have and walk away. This time. Please."

"I can't. I mean not now. I feel like if I do, they'll just pin it on him. He'll go down for the deaths. They can say he felt guilty. He'll be a scapegoat."

"But what if he did do it? Why do you think he didn't?"

"I don't know. He was a MAID doc, doing this work no one else cares about. Or maybe they do care but from a distance; they don't get their hands dirty. And then when there is an issue, when other people disagree, it becomes a problem, a fault. Even if it's not."

"But Rivien, if you are investigating this, you are not being objective. You can't go in with a predetermined solution."

"I'm being a devil's advocate."

"But who are you advocating for?"

"The patient. My whole life it's been the patient."

"It's not your life anymore, Riv. At least, it wasn't supposed to be."

Rivien could feel herself getting flushed. She knew Justin was probably right, but that didn't make it any easier to swallow.

"You're starting to sound like my mom now."

"Thanks."

"You know what I mean. I'm sorry. If you were here, I think I could get you to understand, to help me."

"I did offer to stay, to get a transfer."

"I know. I haven't forgotten."

"Listen, you can call me anytime. You know that. And I am happy to be your sounding board. If there is something I can do to help, I will. But as much as I love solving mysteries with you, I care much more about you not getting hurt, not again."

"Thanks. I'll be careful. It's not like last time. I'm at home, not in the middle of nowhere. I'll keep you posted. I'm sure my role will be over soon. I hope it turns out well, as much as it can now that the doc has died."

"Listen, I want to try to come out for a visit as soon as I can get away. Let me know when you're ready. I'd love to see Rita too, if it's okay. But if you want to wait until your life is less crazy with this contract, I understand."

"I'd love that. I'll call you in a few days."

"I'm going on nights for a bit here. But if you need me, just text, and I'll call you back as soon as I can."

"Sounds good."

"Miss you."

"Miss you too."

And she did. It didn't really change much. It was still too messy, too far, too many memories, and too much uncertainty about the future. But she still missed him.

CHAPTER 19

As she drove, Rivien decided her next stop should be the hospital, and she thought she would run her plan by Priyana.

"What's up, doc?" Priyana said when she picked up.

"Oh, good grief, that's an old one." Rivien was unable to suppress a smile at the silly salutation from the very professional Priyana.

"Thought I'd try something to lighten the mood. You're right, that's a swing and a miss."

"Or at best, a dad joke, and that's below you, lady."

"No argument here. What is your plan today?" asked Priyana.

"I'm going to go to the hospital pharmacy. I'll say my visit is to check on the status of the meds that Josh sped away with yesterday."

"Have they been found and returned to the hospital?"

"I don't think so. Josh may have changed his mind and brought them back before he went home for the last time. But even if that's not likely, I can still pretend I'm checking."

"Good idea."

"And I also want to find out who prepared those medications before they were handed to Josh and me at the hospital pickup. I don't know if it was the same pharmacist that we met with or if someone else did the preparation. There has to be a record, and since I never saw Josh tamper with the meds, and assuming that was one differential diagnosis for the adverse reaction, then the pharmacist preparing them has to be questioned."

"You're right, but I don't know that they'll tell you anything."

"Right, but thanks to you, I was there to witness this whole debacle. I'm going to play it up a bit. It was super upsetting, that's no lie, and I'm going to push the pharmacy team on that. They get to sit up there and mix drugs but they didn't have to see what I saw. I don't mind making them feel it a bit."

"But you also don't want to scare more of them off from MAID, right?"

"Damn you and your reason. Stop trying to rain on my parade. I want to feel like the injured party."

"You laugh, but I know you have every right. I'm not saying don't do it. I actually think it's a good plan. Make sure they get that this wasn't a MAID issue, it was something else, maybe even something sinister. Put some fear in them."

"I like the way you think. Yes, I can do that."

"Keep me posted, okay?"

"I will," Rivien said.

"I have a phone conference with the registrar this morning about Dr. Landry's death and a communication strategy around it. That will be a nightmare."

"Don't envy you. Hope it goes okay. I gotta go now. Talk soon."

As Rivien pulled onto the highway for the short drive to the hospital, she looked around as she dipped into the coulee before rising again to the plateau. The sun was bright today and

Rivien rolled down her window to catch a breath of fresh air. Although she could hear the hum of the other traffic, it did not detract from the surrounding nature; the coulees and their weather-worn facade were in competition with no one. The valley bottom of the coulee was green and lush, even if artificially so. The top plateau was a more natural brush prairie, with hardy low-slung bushes adept at bucking the wind, and prickly cacti ready to defend themselves from errant bikers. Somewhere on the plateau, the rattlesnakes would be sunning themselves on groomed trails, the local inhabitants accustomed to "giving way." It was the middle, the split between the upper land and the lower depths, where the coulees really shone. To many, it probably just looked like sedimentary layers cleaved vertically by eons of water erosion. But to Rivien, the vertical tears through the steadfast time capsule of the coulee's many layers were evidence that, although the work to build a life may be methodical, the fissures that arise from seemingly small droplets are what really shape us. You can lay down foundation, followed by every manner of plan and accomplishment, but what comes along to mold you is rarely within your control. The wrinkles show the pain, but the residual, what is not carved away, shows the resistance. Your final outcome may be less polished, but more real. *Straight lines are for sissies*, Rivien thought as she drove by.

CHAPTER 20

When Rivien arrived at the pharmacy, she was ready for a confrontation with Michael. Although he had a mild-mannered, nerdy, try-hard vibe, she was pretty sure he was a serpent, pouring poison and telling tales outside of school. Her bad luck, of course, that he had called in sick that day.

As she was about to ask for the manager, she spied a friend of hers, Christina, who worked as a pharmacy technician. She flashed her ME letter, which meant nothing there, really (but a confident attitude goes a long way), as she waved at Christina and walked through to the back. An office was open, and Christina gestured her in.

"Did you hear about Josh Landry?" Christina asked.

"Yes, I did. That's why I'm here. I've been asked by the ME to look into a few cases that Josh was involved in. Obviously that focus has changed a bit now."

"Do you mean the MAID case from yesterday? I heard before he died he took off with the MAID drugs. They were all talking about it today, trying to figure out how they should complete the official paperwork."

"Yeah, I know all those cases are monitored and audited, and there is a crazy paper trail. But there were also some questions about earlier cases."

"Yes," confirmed Christina. "I heard that scuttlebutt around here too. They even sent some drugs away to get tested, see if they were tampered with."

"Wow, the news really gets around this office, eh?"

"It's the hospital." Christina laughed. "You remember what it's like. Good gossip spreads faster here than influenza!"

"I suppose. Can I ask you something about a Michael Clubb?"

"That prick. He is the biggest kiss-ass I have ever met, and you can't trust him as far as you can throw him. He is always looking out for number one."

"That was my impression too, but I also wondered if he was trying to curry favor with anyone higher up."

"Do you mean God?"

Rivien laughed. "Well, not actually. I meant his bosses, or maybe administrators here or at Sacrament. But yeah, I guess God too. What makes you say that?"

"He's the biggest God-squad hypocrite you ever met. I get so sick of hearing him talk religion here, putting other people down. I talked to our boss about it once, and I know I wasn't the only one. You know I'm not big on religion, but don't they say 'Judge not lest ye be judged'? That guy judged everyone. No one was up to his high standards."

"I think he has broken confidentiality and probably slandered some people, even in the short time I've been aware of him."

Christina was silent for a minute. "Did you say you are helping the ME? Like, officially?"

"Yeah, I have paperwork, I can show you. I'm under contract."

"No, that's not necessary. I believe you. But what I said about the drugs being tested, you knew that already, right? That is what you are looking into."

"Yeah, that's part of it. Wondering if those meds could have been diverted and implicated in other nonnatural deaths. Why?"

"Well, the day they sent those meds off to be tested, I was working. I wasn't involved, although sometimes techs handle the returns of MAID drugs with a pharmacist. But I knew they were already suspicious from a previous event, so they had a plan to test the ones returned that day. Sarah, the admin, had been sorting out all day how to arrange to send them, since they knew they'd be getting returned after a planned provision."

"Okay, so what do you remember about that day?"

"I remember Dr. Landry coming in. I always thought he was pretty cute, and I think he was single, so I tried to just 'be around' whenever he came in, see if I could chat him up. That day I missed him completely because I had an urgent request. I remember feeling pretty bummed."

Rivien wanted to speed her friend along. As much as she loved some girlie crush chat over wine, this was not the time. *Get to the point, woman!*

"Anyway," continued Christina, "that's why I remember the day. I kind of rushed through my request to see if I could not-so-casually bump into him. And I had just missed him when I heard the panic alarm go off, the one in our department."

"Panic alarm, for what?"

"It's the Code Brown alert in our department, like how emergency has Code Blue alarms? Pharmacy and pathology have Code Brown alarms, so we can pull them and an immediate notification goes to switchboard to announce it."

"Code Brown? You mean like a chemical spill?"

"Yes, or any sort of harmful substance that is uncontrolled. I know you clinical guys like to use it as a euphemism for a diarrhea disaster."

Rivien didn't laugh, although she normally would. You can be a forty-something doctor who still hasn't outgrown potty humor, especially when it's a guaranteed way to get an adorable laugh from a preschooler. "So what happened?"

"The alarm got pulled, so that closes some doors automatically, and then the response team is supposed to get in their hazmat suits and respond. Some of the pharmacy team is on the response team, since we know what the drugs are, and security and environmental services also have designated responders."

"So what was the spill?"

"It was some formaldehyde. We don't even know when it spilled. One of the other techs went into the back supply room and found a bottle tipped over and leaking on the floor. It matters, but it is also one of the most common spills we have in the hospital, so we are pretty well versed at dealing with it. The reason the whole day sticks in my mind is that Michael was the designated pharmacy response member that day, and he was nowhere to be found. The guy who stepped in for him was pretty pissed and made a bit of a scene. And then about fifteen minutes into the event, Michael shows up again, says he was in the washroom."

"Couldn't he have been? Bad timing?"

"Except I saw him come out of the manager's office, not the washroom. I thought at the time he was chickenshit, too afraid to deal with a spill, and so he made someone else do it. I didn't think about it until after, yesterday, when the other MAID meds didn't get returned and everyone was in a tizzy. The office he was hiding in had the MAID meds Dr. Landry had brought back the previous time. The alarm was sounded so shortly after Dr. Landry left that the manager hadn't even had a chance to take them back to disposal, where they were going to package them to send to analysis. And the manager has to be Incident Command if there is ever a full-blown Code Brown, so he went to see what was going on."

"So you're saying Michael, the one who helped raise the suspicions about Dr. Landry, was alone in a room with the meds that were to be sent for testing."

"Yes, but that's not all of it. I also think he might have set the whole Code Brown in motion. When he came out, even though he was supposed to be on the response team, he was the only person who wasn't asking what had happened."

Rivien sat back. Without any proof, or really any way of getting it, she felt certain she knew what happened to those meds in the isolated room. The dilution was a ruse to throw suspicion on Dr. Landry. But why would Michael do that? What did he have against the doctor, aside from a moral disagreement? Would someone really try to get an innocent person suspended, possibly even accused of murder, because of a difference in moral philosophy? But of course it was possible they would. Whole wars had been fought over less. *So stupid.*

"Christina, can I put what you told me into my report for the ME? That's the only place it's going, but someone needs to know what you saw that day. At least if I have it down in my report, they can follow it up later if they need to. I don't know how we'll be able to confirm it, but it needs to go in there."

"Sure," Christina replied. "I don't owe Michael any loyalty. And I've never gotten anywhere bringing my concerns about him to our boss here, so sure, go right ahead. He deserves it."

Rivien knew she still needed to sort out the issue of the meds from the botched MAID case of the previous day. That had been her main intention when she arrived; the new info from Christina was more fuel for the fire.

"Christina, can I talk to one of the pharmacists that would have prepared the MAID drugs for yesterday's provision?"

"I'm pretty sure that was the manager, Anthony Hamish. We have so many objectors, he ends up doing them himself a lot."

Rivien thanked Christina and then went back to pharmacy reception to ask for Anthony again. When she was shown into his office, Rivien was about to say it was nice to see him after their initial meeting with Michael, when Anthony put his hand up in front of her face as she settled into a chair. She immediately saw red and stopped herself from slapping it down.

"Hey!" was all she said.

"Listen," said Anthony coldly. "I know what you are about to ask and don't bother. I have already spoken to our union and also to legal for the health authority. You are not a zone employee, you have no warrant, you are not the cops, and I do not have to talk to you."

Rivien was stunned. He had seemed helpful at their first meeting and now he was radiating malice. Rivien said calmly, "I have been asked by the ME to investigate and I am trying to get to the bottom of what is going on here. Don't forget, it was a member of your department that helped initiate this whole complaint."

"I don't care. I confirmed that a contract ME investigator is not working under judicial authority, and I do not need to answer, certainly not without a union or legal representative present. If the ME has formal questions for me, they may be conveyed to me in writing, and I will review them with my senior director."

"Why are you being like this? Don't you want to know what happened?"

"All I know is that Dr. Landry's inappropriate clinical care led to a patient's awful suffering and the anguish of his family. I am not going to let you pin that on me because he used meds I had prepared and he isn't here to accept the blame."

"None of that is proven. And that is not what we are trying—"

"Stop. I'm asking you to leave. You can dig into his dirt if you want, but you are not taking me down with him."

With that, Anthony turned in his chair, his back to Rivien, who sat there stunned. She eventually stood, but not being one who surrendered the last word easily, she said, "This isn't the end" as she turned to leave. Then she kicked herself for the lame retort and spent the walk to the elevator rehashing what she should have said instead. *Fuck off, you self-centered twat* was all she could come up with. She wasn't convinced that line would have been any better.

CHAPTER 21

Rivien decided her next stop needed to be the hospice, as Karen had told her the antidepressant medications found in Josh's car were from a patient currently admitted there for palliative care. Rivien needed to know how Josh got a hold of them, and if anything like this had ever happened before he knew the powers that be were suspicious of him.

Rivien purposely decided not to call Gerald and let him know she had more questions, and she smiled at the self-righteous indignation she knew he would feel when he found out. She didn't care. She felt very strongly that Gerald and Michael had been conspiring against Josh, and even if they believed they had been vindicated, Rivien was still not sure. She had seen many docs make mistakes, and then proceed to blame everyone else. Other doctors, the nurses, the patients themselves. What she had seen in Josh's face as he sped away from her at the curb was guilt, but also regret. She recognized that combination as humility, not hubris, and she knew he did not take his failure lightly. She had felt that weight, and she felt empathy. What she picked up from Gerald and Michael was judgment, a much dirtier and baser human reaction.

She called Priyana as she drove to the hospice and filled her in on how it had gone down at the hospital pharmacy.

"Mr. Hamish certainly is not working in the spirit of mutual assistance for the benefit of all patients" was Priyana's comment.

"That's a nicer assessment than I made. I may or may not have called him a twat."

"To his face?" Priyana asked, but with a giggle.

"Well, no. In my head. But still, I can talk a good game."

"I am sure that you know how to walk the line between feeling the frustration and actually expressing it."

"I don't know about that," said Rivien. "I definitely liked bitching about doctors I didn't think were pulling their weight."

"But did you tell them? I mean directly?"

"No. You're right, probably more behind their back, or at least in my head behind their back, or even more likely, with passive-aggressive side comments. *Oh, it must be nice to have time to inject filler, you know, instead of seeing patients who actually need you.* I can be a bit of a bitch."

"I doubt that very much. You were very likely right, and I think you are a good judge of character. And I also think you probably kept your true feelings concealed better than you thought."

"I think I need to be liked, and I like to think I'm tougher than I am."

"You are plenty tough, and there is nothing wrong with not wanting to upset people for no reason. I have seen so many doctors in never-ending personal conflict. And I don't mean one snarky comment here or there. I mean fights, and complaints and backstabbing and harassment."

"I've witnessed some of that. It really is shocking. For being filled with smart people, hospitals really can be the Island of Misfit Toys."

"Very true. So do you think you can charm the nurses at the hospice to find out about the missing meds, the ones Karen said were found with Dr. Landry?"

"That's off the record, right? I only told you because I need you to be my sounding board. Don't put that in any reports or anything until it comes from the ME or the cops."

"Absolutely, you have my word. I hope you can find the information you need."

"Me too. Nurses generally like me, at least I think they do, or did. But it's hard to know. Maybe they said I was great and then talked about me behind my back."

"I am sure they didn't and I am sure they won't. I hope you don't mind my saying, but for such a strong person, you really have a fair bit of uncertainty about yourself."

"I don't mind you saying it. You are a good judge of character too. I don't know if it is uncertainty, or constantly feeling like I have to prove myself. I grew up in a high-achieving family. They were great, but being great was assumed, and it wasn't really greatness, it was just being."

"You know you are talking to an Indian mother, correct? I kick myself at night sometimes, thinking about the expectations I put on my children, even if I didn't mean to."

"I hear you. My family made me strong and competent. I wish they made me better able to believe it myself. What a trip that must be! Anyway, I'm here. We'll chat later, I'll let you know how it goes."

Rivien parked, entered the hospice, and took the elevator to the third floor. As the doors opened, she strode forward without thinking and bumped straight into Nurse Pike entering the elevator.

"Shit, sorry," Rivien said, while the upright and proper nurse gave her a glare but stopped short of clutching her cross necklace.

"Dr. Gilrie. What are you doing here? Are you meeting Mr. Strong?"

"Not really. I need to check on something. I suppose you heard about what happened to Dr. Landry?"

"God rest his soul. I will pray for him and hope he finds peace."

"That is very kind. I want to follow up some leads, some questions about him. I want to get to the bottom of why he did what he did."

"Of course, but I don't know that we will ever understand what makes someone take a life, especially their own. Inner demons are not understandable to others, and are the hardest evil to fight."

For whatever reason, Rivien found the statement comforting. The recognition that we all fight battles, and that outside recrimination is not helpful. "Do you think I could ask you some questions, Nurse Pike?"

"Of course. And Margaret is fine, dear. No matter what Dr. Landry had or had not done, he was a kind soul and he deserves whatever assistance I may be able to offer."

Rivien had been holding the elevator-open button during their exchange, and released it as Margaret signaled to follow her down the hall into the peaceful family room. As the two women got settled with fresh cups of coffee, Rivien considered her best approach.

"I need to request that what I ask you stays between us. There will be an official investigation of Dr. Landry's death, but I am helping the ME gather some information that may assist."

"I understand and can assure you that I know how to keep a confidence."

"I have no doubt, and thank you. I'm going to come out with it. Some pills were found at Dr. Landry's house, in his car actually, and the police have already confirmed the name on the bottle matches a patient who is currently admitted here."

"I am sorry to say that yes, of this I was aware. Some of my younger colleagues are not the very souls of discretion, and I heard gossip regarding this fact when I arrived today. Apparently, an investigator had phoned during the night shift and confirmed this fact."

"Yeah, shit gets around in a hospital, that's for sure," Rivien said and then inwardly winced at her continued casual profanity in front of the matronly nurse. "Anyway, do you have any idea when Josh could have taken the medications? He'd been suspended for at least a few days before I even got the case."

"Yes. Well," Margaret said. She fell silent, crossed her hands in her lap, and for the first time looked away from Rivien.

"Sorry," said Rivien, immediately feeling the atmosphere in the room change, not cool but rather slow, as though thoughts and information now needed to be rationed. She could feel Margaret had info to share, the way she had felt with patients right before they disclosed a horrible trauma or abuse. She could taste the reticence, and it fueled her hunger to know more. "What is it, Margaret? You can tell me. Confidentiality goes both ways. I can withhold your identity, to the absolute best of my ability, but if you have anything to tell me, please do."

Margaret sat still, and this time her hand did go to the gold cross around her neck. And then she straightened more, which Rivien did not think possible, and her resolve became a force that Rivien could feel radiate from her.

"Before the police called last night, Mr. Strong had already called the nurses on shift. I was informed of this at handover this morning."

"What was he calling about? He really shouldn't have been talking about Dr. Landry until anything was official."

"My feelings exactly. I don't like back chatter. Regardless, the nurse on shift last night heard of Dr. Landry's death from Mr. Strong. He called her to say the police might be calling and that she had permission from the institution to answer their questions completely."

"Really? Was he not concerned about confidentiality and warrants? Did he think they were going to ask about the unexplained deaths at the facility?"

"No. The nurse said he specifically said that she should answer any questions about current patients truthfully, but refrain from speaking of former patients and refer those questions to him. I found it very strange, as did the nurse who reported it to me. She said the direction was very *pointed*, her word."

"So when the cops did call, did they ask about the pills that were found, and about that patient?"

"Yes, that is exactly what happened and that is why it stuck out in my colleague's mind. It was as if Mr. Strong had known the question would be coming."

"But maybe that was because the cops had asked him already? I am not sure if you are aware, but it was Gerald that sent the cops to Josh's house, to check on him. So if he told them who he was and why he was calling, maybe they already asked him that question, but he needed the nurse to confirm the answer, or clarify specifics."

"Perhaps. And that is a reasonable hypothesis," Margaret said blankly.

"You do not sound convinced."

"Because I am not. The other nurse confirmed the patient's admission date and name and did also confirm for the police that the patient was admitted approximately thirty hours before Dr. Landry's suspension took effect. In fact, Dr. Landry had rounded on that patient the morning before his suspension took effect."

"That is kind of damning."

"It would have been, had all nurses been lax with details. I pride myself on knowing my patients; my charting is impeccable and I accept nothing less. As soon as the information was relayed to me this morning, I knew immediately it was not complete and in my first break, I checked my own charting on that patient. Although the patient had been admitted the day before Dr. Landry was suspended, the family had not brought in the patient's outside medications until the following day."

"What do you mean?" Rivien asked, although she was already putting the pieces together in her mind.

"The bottle reportedly found at Dr. Landry's was clearly from an outpatient pharmacy. Inpatients in a facility are never given a bottle supply of medication; they are supplied daily medication doses as ordered. You yourself know this is true. However, we do request families to bring in medications from home, either to verify the best possible medication profile or occasionally to use as medication in hospital if the medication is back-ordered or not covered by hospital pharmacy."

"So the TCAs were the patient's home supply? Brought in for medication reconciliation."

"Correct. And more importantly, they arrived several hours after Dr. Landry was suspended and he was no longer present in the building. I have it documented in my notes that although the medication profile was completed on admission, I needed to reverify once the home medications arrived. And I did that and documented it again, several hours after the suspension took effect."

Rivien was quiet. This small inconsistency could have easily escaped all notice, if not for this alert nurse. And not only that, she had meticulously documented it in the official record as well. *God bless this woman and her white hat.* "Margaret, this is important. Is there any way Josh could have come back in the building after his suspension?"

"No. I know his key card access was canceled and an official notification came out to all floors that his privileges were presently suspended. It would have been noticed had he been present, as everyone was talking about it. I am sure the medications went missing after Dr. Landry had permanently left the premises. It is why I agreed to speak with you. Why I am glad you are here and found me first. I know I am correct, but what I cannot understand, cannot accept, is why anyone would want to perpetuate this fallacy."

CHAPTER 22

The two women sat quietly, Rivien making plans in her head. *Get a copy of the charting from Margaret, before it can be bastardized or tampered with. Get contact information for the family, so they can verify when the medications were delivered. Call Karen because someone is lying, and the police need to know.* As she was running her mental list, she hadn't noticed Margaret stand and move to a far wall, until she began speaking.

"I've been a nurse for forty-five years. I was with the Daughters of Faith for many years, nursing alongside the nuns, in hospitals overseen by priests or ministers. I have missed only eleven Sunday services in my life, even if many that I attended were in the hospital chapel. I am not exaggerating. A few I missed for the births of my children and only once because I was away on vacation and couldn't find a nearby parish."

Rivien could see that although Margaret was looking away from her, her eyes were focused on the wall in front of her. Rivien stood to join her.

"I always considered myself a wife and mother first, then a Catholic, and then a nurse. But that is not to say that I do not give my full self to nursing; I live for my patients and to serve God by serving them. It is my calling. I prayed when MAID became legal in this country, I cried and prayed for so long. Nothing in my career has shaken my belief so mightily."

"I am sure," said Rivien, placing a hand on the nurse's bony, rigid shoulder. "I know not everyone believes in it; I really do understand that. And I also know it's not perfect, and needs to be very carefully monitored. And I respect people's right to choose for themselves, including what they will do as a medical professional."

"It is not that," Margaret said, "although I know many assume it is."

Rivien held space.

"It is that I knew it was needed. I knew it was righteous. I knew that my church, my friends and family, and even often I myself, could not understand it. But I knew my God believed. My God was tired of the suffering, even if many of those in His church were not hearing His will. I was tired of the suffering. I had seen so much. So many cries in the night. Held so many hands in a death I would not wish on a rat."

Rivien was stunned. This moral, upright woman was struggling. Rivien could not imagine the dissonance, the justifications and recriminations, she must have felt over the short time the MAID option had been available in Canada.

"I am so happy, so pleased to hear your obvious support for patients," Rivien said, carefully considering her words. "I've never heard a devout person speak like this. I usually get Bible verses, or something about hell, or slogans about how all life is precious."

"Those people have not seen death the way I have," Margaret replied. "Not forty-five years of it. Staying present, not turning away. I was like them so much of my life, but I changed, I learned. I saw. A year or so ago, I saw our first patient transferred out of this facility to get a MAID provision. He was in pain but had to be lucid, so he was refusing sedation. He was loaded into an ambulance, in a stretcher, and driven away from us. He was crying, his whole family was crying. The ambulance had been four hours late, called away by another case. The patient was beside himself that he might have to suffer another day, live in fear another day. I cried as he was taken away from me. I had sworn to care for him, he was my patient. And instead he was taken away in the most horrible way. I will never be able to be the one to push the needle, but I don't have to. I could still have been the one to hold his hand, even if his choice would not have been mine, because he was my patient. And in forty-five years I have never turned my back on a patient. That day I did, because this place made me. I will never forget it."

Margaret was crying now, as was Rivien. Together stood two women, two very different women, but still two healers. Two healers broken by a system which had made them confront their failings, and then soldier on while the powers that be continued in blind ignorance of the suffering in their wake. Rivien had gotten out, but Margaret's calling was too pure.

"It was not your fault, or your choice," said Rivien, thinking back to all of her patients, desperate for the choice to control their own lives and bodies, trapped in a maze of refusals and stigma. "It was a will imposed on you, and your patient. I am so sorry this happened, is still happening."

"As am I. My only grace is that I know I am right with God; he does not wish this on his people. I know who does—those who think they speak for God. That is at whose feet the blame lies." She turned her head again to focus on a large framed photo on the wall. Two rows of people dressed in suits, with a few men in clerical robes also present. To Rivien's quick count there were fourteen men and only one woman in the photo. It had been taken outside, and Rivien recognized the statue in the background as the one that stood in the courtyard next to the Sacrament facility. An engraved brass plaque identified those pictured as the *Board of Governors, Saint Michael's Health Facility, Sacrament Health, 2022.*

Rivien recognized at least a half dozen faces, many of whom she had not realized had any connection to Sacrament. Rivien stared hard at the faces and wondered how many were staring back with judgment; Margaret crossed herself.

CHAPTER 23

Rivien called Priyana as she left the hospice. "You won't believe it, but someone is lying about the meds. Josh didn't have an opportunity to steal them. They weren't even in the hospice until he was gone."

"How do you know that?" said Priyana, her voice ramping up with excitement, matching Rivien's.

"That nurse, remember, Nurse Pike? She told me. She has notes, it's all documented."

"Did you get copies? I know it is official charting, but what if something happens to it?"

"That's what I thought! I was worried about the same thing. But I don't have a warrant, so I can't actually remove anything from the building, and people don't even have to answer my questions. But Margaret said she would take copies herself, store them in her locker. They will not leave the building, and she will destroy her copies once the police come to get the originals and she can ensure nothing was changed."

"She'd do that? Isn't she afraid she will be reprimanded? Do you trust her?"

"I do trust her, I really do. She is upset with how things are being done in Sacrament. She is conflicted, but she is too strong to let anyone tell her what is best for her patients, or her faith. She's pretty cool."

"Yes, I got that impression, but she has really changed the course here. Someone is hiding something, probably someone at Sacrament."

"It has to be Gerald," said Rivien.

"I don't know that we can jump to that conclusion. It could be anyone with access to that building. And it doesn't completely clear Josh, since he could have been involved with someone there."

"I know you're right. But I get a bad feeling about the whole place. Not the people, not most of them, but the place."

"I know. Have you called the police?" Priyana asked, gently directing Rivien back to solutions, away from suspicion.

"I am calling Karen next, and I will get her contact at the police, find out who is investigating Josh's death. I'll get on it right away."

"I've been able to extend my time here. I can do some of my work remotely, so the College doesn't really need to know where I am until I am reassigned to another investigation. I got them to assign me to an infection prevention and control follow-up at a clinic here in town, so that should take a day or so."

"That's great. Let's get a drink tonight. Come and sit on my deck, and we'll see what we can sort out."

"Sounds good, keep me posted."

As Rivien walked to her car after relaying all the new information to Karen, she decided to call Edi again. The case was starting to look more criminal, or at least more complicated, and her sister had experience with criminal cases in spades. Edi had told her to extricate herself, but now she could show her why she couldn't; there was something here, but she needed help determining next steps.

"Hey, how's it going? Did you hand off your case?" asked Edi, who picked up her phone on the third ring.

"Not exactly. I was going to chase down some medications, something that was found at the scene of the doctor's death, and—"

"Rivien!"

"Just wait, I need your help. There is some fakakta stuff happening here."

"What else is new? The whole world is fakakta. Tell me fast, I've got a meeting in fifteen minutes."

"I went to the hospital but got stonewalled at the pharmacy. I think they know there is going to be a family complaint about that MAID provision that went terribly wrong, and since they provided the meds, they are covering their collective asses."

"I thought they'd be trying to throw blame at the doctor who died."

"Oh, there was some of that too, but so far no one has found the MAID meds he took home with him. They also can't clear themselves, so it's official duck and cover right now. But the bigger issue is that there were meds found in Dr. Landry's car, ones that might have contributed to the suicide. The cops already found out, through the Sacrament manager, the one that initiated the complaint, that the drugs were missing from the hospice. So he tried to imply Josh stole them. It turns out Josh couldn't have stolen them from the hospice. They were removed after he was suspended, so we don't know how they got in his car."

"Holy fuck," said Edi. "That changes things, Riv. You need to tread carefully here. Are you implying that someone gave them to Josh, to encourage the suicide?"

"No, that wasn't my thought. I was wondering if someone could have planted them."

"Whoa. Hold on. You don't plant drugs at the scene of a suicide. So, if—and it's a big if—you think there is any chance the suicide was staged, then this may have been a murder, not a suicide."

"I don't know. I don't know anything for sure, but what if that's true? I already called Karen. She is calling the cops as we speak. The autopsy is done, but there were no injuries to be found, so they are waiting on the tox screen. Alcohol level was through the roof, but testing for the TCAs takes longer. She can confirm that carbon monoxide is what actually killed him."

"But you're wondering if someone drugged him?"

"I guess so. He was a pretty fit dude, but if he was drunk enough, maybe someone could have helped things along and then got him into the car."

"The police need to check that car and the pill bottle for prints. They might not have done that if they were still thinking suicide."

"I know. Karen said the car was impounded, the house was still cordoned off, and they have the med bottle in evidence. So they are going to process that as soon as possible."

"Who would have done this?" Edi asked. "You told me he had the brutal MAID death—or not death—that day, but would the family have really gone out and got revenge that fast?"

"I really doubt it. They were pissed, of course, but I don't know how they would even know where to find him. I'm more concerned about Gerald Strong, the hospice manager. Not only was he the one who put in the complaint, but he was also the one who reportedly called the cops to Josh's place. He said it was a wellness check, but that is too fucking convenient."

"Would he have had access to the drugs?"

"They were at his facility, not that he should have been wandering into patient rooms, but who knows?"

"Could he have drugged the doc? Do you know if they saw each other that night?"

"As far as I heard, no, he only tried to call Josh and got no answer. I don't think they were drinking buddies or anything.

I wouldn't be having beers with the guy who was trying to get me canned."

"But why would Gerald kill Josh? He'd already put the College and the ME onto Josh, so why would he want to finish him off?"

"I have no idea. They were on different sides of the MAID issue stuff, but that would be no reason to kill him. It's too far of a stretch."

"The cops need to interview him, for sure," Edi said.

"What are you suggesting? I can't call them up and order that. I am a bossy broad, but I am aware that, despite my meager efforts, I am still not a cop."

"I know, smart-ass. It's not for you to order. But your ME friend can light a fire. You already gave all this info to her, so is there really anything else you can do?"

"No, I don't think so. The cases I was asked to investigate aren't cleared, but I don't think they ever really will be with Josh gone. But this is way crazier now."

"In all seriousness, Riv, you need to be careful. There is a very real chance this was not a straightforward suicide. Even if it wasn't murder, someone is trying to paint a picture, spin the scene and the story in a way that plays out well for them. Those people start to make mistakes, and when they dig themselves in deeper, they get dangerous."

"I know. I'm not going anywhere near any of it now. I am literally just going to look at some charts and try to chase down the lab work on the MAID meds that got sent for testing. I managed to get some records from the hospice preserved today, so that was good. I think I work on this another day, maybe two, and then kick it back to Karen and the cops. I doubt I even have to leave the house to work on this anymore."

"Sounds good. Keep me posted. I want to know when you are done, okay?"

"Yes, my learned friend, okay."

"Screw you. Love you."

"Love you too."

CHAPTER 24

That night Rivien and Rita built a snap-together birdhouse that they painted a cacophony of colors.

"I don't think we need the rhinestones, Nugget," said Rivien, trying to rein in the ever-expanding craft project, especially as bedtime approached.

"Yes, we do. I want fancy birds to live here. They need gems," Rita said.

"They might try to eat the gems, and the birds could choke."

"They don't choke. They will like how fancy it is. Maybe the Queen Bird will come to live with us."

"That would be cool. A Queen Bird."

"Yes, and she will lay babies. Babies love sparklies," Rita said with assurance, pressing more gems into the smear of white glue sliding slowly down the wall of the birdhouse.

It must be nice to be so sure of things all the time, thought Rivien. *When do we learn to start questioning ourselves all the time? Where does that come from?*

"I'm sure you're right, Nugget. Why wouldn't they? The birds will love anything you build."

"I love you, Mama."

"I love you too. Always will. But now it's time for bed. You go potty, wash your hands, and I'll get this cleaned up a bit. I'll come help you with your teeth."

"Show?"

"Not tonight. Tomorrow is preschool, and we did the craft instead of a show tonight, remember?"

Rita nodded. "But we read a story?"

"Yes, we have time for a story. Now go potty, and I'll be right there."

Rita bounced off and Rivien winced and smiled as she left a tiny purple handprint on the wall as she turned into the hall. Rivien tidied up the craft area and removed the incriminating evidence from the wall. *So thankful for washable paint. So blessed by tiny hands.*

After Rivien had tucked Rita in and read a chapter in their dragon-themed book, she turned on the noise machine and the light projector, ensured all appropriate stuffed animals were in attendance in her daughter's bed, and finally turned off the light. As she closed the door, she could hear Rita recounting the events of her day to a favored stuffie, a blue dragon with burgundy wings. He had been loved so hard in four short years that he looked like he had been in a war. *Oh, if only everyone in the world could experience a tenth of the love that dragon felt,* Rivien thought.

Priyana had texted that she was on her way over for a drink and strategy session. Rivien put a bottle of Pinot in the fridge to give it a bit of a chill, but then remembered she had left her notepad in her car in the garage. She grabbed her purse; her car had a proximity lock and the keys were in her purse.

The notebook was on the floor on the passenger side in the back, probably not the most secure place for it. Rivien chided herself for her carelessness, now that she was back in charge of confidential information again. When she slipped her hand under the door handle, something stung her and she immediately jerked her hand back again.

"Shit!" She saw a pinpoint spot of blood start to rise on her fourth finger pad. "What the hell?" she said as she leaned way down to look under the handle. Her car had lighted door handles, and she recoiled when she saw the source of her injury. Wedged up under her handle was a small syringe and an exposed hypodermic needle.

CHAPTER 25

"Jesus Christ," Rivien said as she slouched back onto her butt. She never meant to be disrespectful to others by taking the Lord's name in vain, but he wasn't her Lord anyway and at this juncture, she didn't fucking care.

She sat like that for several minutes, slowing her breathing and trying to think what to do next. She got up and grabbed a pair of old gloves from a basket and a clean pickle jar out of her recycling. Then she changed her mind. This was not like finding a discarded needle in an alley. Rivien was totally comfortable safely removing such debris herself, with no need to call the local needle response team. This was different.

There was zero chance this needle had been accidently discarded here. It had been carefully placed and wedged in securely while still leaving the business end pointed directly in harm's way. Rivien took out her phone and took some pictures. When she called the police nonemergency line, it took her several minutes to convince them she was not calling because she was some sheltered whiner who was terrified of discarded drug paraphernalia.

"No," she said again, "I am not asking the police to come and pick up a needle. I am asking them to come and investigate an assault." *Good grief,* she thought; she might have to call Edi to get this across to them. Finally, when she had it sorted and after agreeing to wait "until an officer is free," she hung up.

She knew what her next call needed to be, having made similar calls many times before during her work with the sexual assault response team at the hospital. Rivien was not prone to panic, although she was inclined to overthinking and paralysis by analysis. She tried her best to be guided by science and logic, but she couldn't ignore the fact that any blood and body fluid exposure carried a certain level of risk. She was about to call the familiar number for the on-call medical officer of health when her own phone rang.

"Rivien, I'm at your front door. You're upstairs, above the wine shop, correct? I didn't want to ring the bell if your little one was probably asleep."

"Shit."

"Excuse me?"

"Sorry, sorry, Priyana, hold on, I'll buzz you in. But I'm actually out back, in the garage. Something has happened. Come up through the apartment and down the back stairs. I'll show you."

"Show me what? Are you okay? You sound…different."

"Yes, I'm okay. Come down."

When Priyana opened the door to the garage she called Rivien's name, unable to see her still sitting on the dirty cement floor beside her car.

"I'm over here, Priyana."

"For goodness' sake, what are you doing on the floor?" Priyana spoke lightly until she saw Rivien's face: pale, fighting back tears, but angry at the same time. "My god, Rivien. Are you hurt?"

"I'm okay, but come look at this." Rivien pointed up toward the underside of the door handle while moving her head to the side. As Priyana leaned down, her hand extended out of habit and Rivien barked, "Don't touch it!"

"Is that a needle, a syringe? What in the world is that doing there? Did you touch it?"

"Yeah, unfortunately."

"Did it poke you? Oh, Rivien."

"Yep, I grabbed it full on when I went to open the car door."

"Who would do such a thing?"

"Exactly. It can't have been an accident. Do you think there is any chance this could be related to the case?"

"I don't think so, I hope not, but what if it is? Rivien, this is serious. Something is terribly wrong here. Have you called the police?"

"Yes, just before you got here. They are sending someone."

"Did you explain about the case, about the suspicion?"

"Not really, it was dispatch, but I will. At least that I am doing an investigation. But this is crazy. Priyana, it was the passenger side, in the back." Rivien stopped. "Whoever did this didn't put the needle under my door, they put it on a back door."

"Your daughter!" Priyana gasped.

"You can see the booster seat through the windows. If they wanted to hurt me, wouldn't they put it under my door? If this was related to the case, what if someone put it there to hurt Rita?" Now the tears fell.

"Oh, Rivien," Priyana said as she dropped gracefully to the ground and wrapped Rivien in a hug. Her arms were thin but Rivien felt their power and knew they had comforted many. Rivien cried into a shoulder much wider in spirit than in reality.

"They weren't trying to hurt me. It did, but there would be much worse ways…" Rivien's voice trailed off as she thought of her past and the nearly fatal attack she had suffered at the hands of an anti-choice zealot. "They wanted to scare me, hurt my family, or at least show me they could."

"I'm so sorry. Don't worry, we can take care of you. We can make sure nothing bad comes of this exposure. I am so thankful it was you that found it, not Rita," Priyana said as she held Rivien.

"Me too. You wouldn't believe the luck. When I picked her up today, there was no room on the street by the preschool, so I went around the corner onto a one-way street and parked on the left. She got in the back driver-side door. Otherwise she might have gotten to the needle before me."

"When do you think it was put there?"

"It had to be today, sometime after I dropped her off. This morning I was parked the other way. That always puts us on the right side of the road at drop-off."

"Where were you today?"

"I ran a few errands, but the hospital and the hospice were the only places I was parked for a while."

"Rivien, you need to tell the police about the ME investigation. If you can't disclose everything, then tell them they need to talk to Dr. Pinder. I don't believe this was an accident; too coincidental. And you need to call someone about testing, or medications, for yourself. I haven't had to do that for many years. Not too many needle sticks in psychiatry."

"We had to call the medical officer of health about blood and body fluid exposures all the time for the sexual assault response team. I've got the on-call number still saved in my phone."

"Okay, why don't you call them while we wait for the police. Come on upstairs, where it is more comfortable."

"You know, I think I'll stay down here. I know it's silly, but chain of custody and all that. I'll call from here, and hopefully the police won't be long. But can you go upstairs and make yourself comfortable. If Rita happens to get up or anything, just holler for me. Right now I want someone up there with her."

"Of course. And I will find your kettle and your tea bags and there will be hot tea waiting for you when you come up."

"I think I'd rather have a glass of wine...or maybe a bottle."

"Talk to the MOH first. And maybe alcohol isn't the best idea right now."

"You're right, but I'm probably going to do it anyway."

"Well, then, I might raid your liquor cabinet instead, see what you have to add to that tea."

"Deal. And Priyana..."

"Yes?"

"Thank you for being here. I'm really glad you are."

"Absolutely, my dear. Me too. We will get to the bottom of this. I have a feeling they messed with the wrong lady."

As Priyana headed for the door, Rivien looked again at the needle. *They fucking well did,* she thought.

CHAPTER 26

Rivien sat back on her dirty garage floor, facing the offending car door and willing herself to stay calm. She called the MOH number and was prompted to leave a voice mail, after a greeting that stated that Dr. Prottus was on call and would call back within thirty minutes. Rivien was grateful, as she knew and trusted Dr. Prottus, but she was still overwhelmed by anger and hatred.

Since welcoming Rita into her life, everything else for her had shifted. Nothing mattered other than giving Rita the love and life that she deserved, that every child deserves. The idea that someone would come after an innocent child hardened Rivien to a degree that her neck began to go into spasm and her chest grew cold from the inside out. If this attack on everything she held dear was at all related to her current case, whoever did this was going to live to regret it. Rivien had already put one man in the ground for shattering her world; she knew she would do it again if required.

"Hello. This is Dr. Prottus, MOH on call, returning a call."

"Hi, Dr. Prottus. It's Dr. Gilrie. Sorry to call you direct. I realized as I dialed I really should have gone through the switchboard."

"That's okay. Health-care workers can call me directly, that's no issue."

"I'm actually calling for myself, I'm the patient this time. So I apologize."

"Don't worry about it, I remember your name from SART. What can I do for you?"

"About fifteen minutes ago I got a needle stick injury."

"At work? Did you give occupational health and safety a call?"

"Actually, no. It's a bit complicated. I'm retired from being a doctor. So the stick happened at home. But it's a bit weirder than your standard poked-myself-with-some-garbage-outside issue."

"All right," said Dr. Prottus slowly but blankly, apparently wondering what kind of crazy situation she was about to encounter. Rivien knew from experience that docs are pretty much ready for any story. After seeing every possible manner of item put in every conceivable bodily orifice with every imaginable justification, you become immune to the quirks of the human species.

"I know the risk is probably low, but this was a small-bore needle, syringe attached, that was jammed up under my car door handle."

"Like someone put it there on purpose?"

"Yes, I have to believe so. I have already called the cops, and they're going to come look into it."

"That's terrible, I'm so sorry. Any idea how it got there?"

"It could have been anyone, some asshole. But I am doing some work for the ME right now, an investigation. And it's probably unrelated, but I've never had anything like this happen before."

"An investigation?"

"Yes, into some unexplained deaths."

"Is this about the doctor that committed suicide? I heard about that, very sad."

"Sort of. He was actually the subject of the concern about the unexplained deaths I was looking into. But then he died. And please don't repeat this, but it is not confirmed to be suicide yet. And there's some strange stuff happening, so I am on edge. And now this. I don't want to believe someone would target me, but I don't know for sure."

"So there may, possibly, have been some malice here. Some intent to harm."

"Maybe, I don't know. But yeah, I'm a bit worried."

"Was there blood or fluid visible in the syringe? Did the poke draw blood on you?"

"No and yes. I didn't see anything in the syringe itself, and it did draw a bit of blood."

"Were you wearing gloves?"

Rivien recognized many of the questions the doctor was asking. The process of risk stratification was a mix of art and science. She had witnessed patients freaking out over exposures to inadvertent needle sticks or low-risk communicable disease exposures, and then voluntarily partaking in far riskier activities on a regular basis. Rivien had always thought it came down to accountability. We love to blame others for the misfortunes that befall us, and we do not like to accept responsibility for the mess we create for ourselves.

"No, no gloves."

"You have any idea where the needle could have come from?"

"No. I was parked over at St. Mike's for some of the day, so I'm guessing maybe it happened there. I can't remember exactly when I last used that door, but I think it was probably this morning."

"I know you know about these things. Do you know what you want to do?"

"Honestly, my brain is mush right now. I'm so glad that my daughter didn't find this, and so furious that she could have. I'm open to your expert advice. What do you think I should do?"

"Well, seems to be a deliberate thing, but we don't know if the aim was to hurt you, or maybe scare you…"

"Mission accomplished."

"Anyway, this wasn't random. I think the precautionary principle in this case would be for you to go on PEP, the HIV post-exposure prophylaxis."

"Damn!" Rivien exclaimed. "But I know you're right. I've never had to take it before."

"The new drugs aren't near as bad as they used to be. It's for a month, and most people do pretty well. There are usually two blood tests, for monitoring. The risk is low, but…"

"But, indeed. What about hepatitis C?"

"We don't prophylax for that, but I will arrange all your testing. Curative treatments are pretty good now, so hopefully it doesn't come to that, but if it does, we will make sure you can get easy access. What about hep B? Do you know if you are immune?"

"Yes, I am. Had those titers all confirmed in med school."

"If this was some run-of-the-mill poke with an outside needle, no idea how long it had been there, I would generally advise against the meds. But given it was intentional and potentially targeted, there is a real chance it was a fresh needle. I don't mean this to scare you, but if someone really was targeting you, they could have picked a source needle that they knew contained a pathogen."

"Fuck," said Rivien. "Sorry." She was as guilty as others. She'd done some stupid stuff, and some even stupider guys, in her younger days, and yet now, through no fault of her own, she had to face the fear of a low-risk exposure to a lifelong, but generally no longer life-limiting, disease like HIV. She understood how her stressed-out patients probably felt. "Okay, if you think I need it, I'll take it."

"Right. I'll set up the blood work and the baseline testing. Can you go to emergency right away and get started on the

PEP? I'll call ahead so they will release it to you. The earlier the better."

"I can go in a little bit. My little girl is asleep upstairs. I have a friend who can stay with her, but I am waiting for the cops too. But I could get my friend to let them in, so they can either find me in emerg if they need a statement, or I might even beat them back here."

"Sounds good. You shouldn't have to wait too long at emerg. I'll take your number and I'll call you with any results. There really isn't a good way to test the needle for pathogens; any blood will be too degraded to test but can still carry virus. So if the police want it for the investigation, that would be more valuable."

"Okay," said Rivien, and after exchanging information, they hung up.

Rivien went upstairs to update Priyana on the plan.

"Yes, of course," Priyana said. "I will let the police in, show them what they need. Here, you take my car." She handed her keys to Rivien.

"I can get a cab."

"Don't be silly, take my car. I will stay here, and if Rita happens to wake I will call you, so she won't be scared of a stranger in her house."

"She's pretty adaptable. She'd probably drag you back to bed with her to read another dragon story."

"I would love that, and I will try not to go in there to watch your little angel sleep."

"Not gonna lie, I'm probably going to crawl in with her tonight when I get back. I need to feel her near me."

"She is in good hands with Nani Priyana. You go and look after yourself and I will deal with the police if they get here first."

"Depending how late I am, maybe we can still chat when I'm back, although I probably won't have a glass of wine with the HIV meds. And I really, really, really need one," Rivien said, trying hard not to cry.

"We won't let them get away with this, Rivien," Priyana said, confirming their mutual feeling that this was not an accident, it was a message. She hugged Rivien, who drank up the support, her only calming solace in a terrible night.

CHAPTER 27

When Rivien returned from the hospital it was getting late, but the cop had arrived. Rivien met the officer and Priyana in the garage as she pulled Priyana's car up outside behind the cruiser.

"Hi, Rivien, this is Officer Barker. He just got here. I let him in, and he's taken some photos so far."

"Thanks for coming," Rivien said. She knew it was his job to come, but it was habit—Canadians always be thanking.

"Can you tell me again when you discovered the needle?" asked Officer Barker, flipping open his little notebook and getting down to business.

Rivien replayed the incident for the officer and explained how that led to her going to the hospital for the medications.

"Where were you parked today? And when was the last time you used that door, before this happened?"

"Well," Rivien said, trying to figure out which question to answer first, "I can't guarantee when I last used that door, but I would say it was likely early this morning. I'm pretty sure I used it to let my kid out at school this morning. But then I might not have used that door again. After preschool, I went to the hospital. I was there for a bit, then I went to the hospice, over at St. Mike's. I grabbed a few groceries before I did the pickup at preschool. We came straight back here, to this garage."

"Were you in the staff lots? At the hospital and at St. Mike's?"

"I'm not staff. I was parked in the visitor lot by the main doors at the hospital, and out front on the street at St. Mike's. I remember because I made some calls walking out to my car. I was standing in the front garden at St. Mike's and watching my car so I wouldn't get a ticket."

"Got it. I'm going to collect this needle now. Take it for evidence. Any prints will be more useful off the syringe itself. Anyone can argue that they touched a car door in public, so prints from that, when it is parked on a public street, are not as useful."

Rivien looked at Priyana, not sure if that was a justification, or an excuse.

Wearing gloves, Officer Barker collected the syringe with the needle and placed it in a plastic evidence bag. But then, looking around, he seemed to realize that would not be a safe option. He rummaged in his kit but only had small plastic bottles for hairs or other trace evidence, and nothing that would fit the needle.

"Here. Want this?" Rivien asked, proffering the clean pickle jar she had previously selected from her recycling.

"Um, I guess," the cop said. "I'll put the whole bag in here. To not contaminate the evidence. Thanks."

After writing Rivien's contact information in his notepad, he promised to have someone call her in the morning, to arrange a time to come to the station to make an official statement.

As they watched the cop pull away, Priyana put a firm arm around Rivien's shoulders, and Rivien was again grateful for her new friend's apparently strong sense of Rivien's mental, if not physical, exhaustion.

"If you're okay, I'm going to head out. We'll connect tomorrow sometime," Priyana said. "You rest, take it easy."

"Thanks, Priyana, and thanks again for being here."

Despite the late hour, Rivien knew someone who would still be up, and with whom she really did want to talk. She had not been buoyed by the level of interest shown by Officer Barker. She had thought about calling Justin, but it was even later out east, and Rivien realized that might put Justin in a difficult position, expecting him to confirm that some other cop wasn't doing his job. So Rivien called Edi. Edi had made a career of confronting not only criminals, but police as well.

"So I think I am in over my head," began Rivien.

"Now what?" asked Edi, concern, and not the usual sarcasm, creeping into her voice.

"Someone planted a needle, a syringe, under my car door handle today."

"What!"

"Yeah, so I poked myself and now I'm on HIV meds. I'm sure this wasn't an accident; someone put it there on purpose. And not only that, they put it under a back door handle, so they were maybe targeting Rita."

"What the fuck, Riv. Is this about the investigation?" Edi asked.

"I don't know."

"It is, isn't it? Do the cops know?"

"Yes, they came to get the needle, but I don't know if they will be able to find anything out."

"I'm coming down."

"You don't have to do that, Edi."

"I'm coming down. They need to find who did this. And I need to see my sister, and my niece. Fuck, this is too much, I'm not letting this go any further. I'm coming down tonight."

"It's too late. Come in the morning."

"What are you doing tomorrow? I don't want you doing anything without me," Edi stated.

"I'll take Rita to preschool. I have to go to the police station later, to make a formal statement."

"Don't do that until I am there. I'll leave around six, and I'll be there by ten-ish. I can see Rita when she gets off school, but I will meet you before you go to the station. Got it?"

"Got it. And Edi, thanks. I can't believe I got mixed up in this kind of shit again."

"It's not your fault. But we end it now, understood?" She hung up without giving Rivien a chance to protest. Rivien would have only feigned resistance anyway; she was glad her little sister was coming.

CHAPTER 28

Rivien took the morning to work in the shop while waiting for Edi to arrive. She must have left early in the morning, as she arrived by 9:30 with what was probably the third coffee of the day in hand.

"No offense, sis," Edi said, "but I thought all this physical peril and my constant stress about you was going to end when you quit working as a doctor. I wanted to hear nothing except boring-ass wine talk, and yet here we are again."

"I know. But this time, I don't know who did this, or why. What the hell does coming after me accomplish? I'm glad I have your help. I have a really strong feeling that nothing much is going to come of this if we don't stay on it."

"Fuckers!" said Edi, not as an indictment of policing, just as her most common utterance. Rivien was glad Rita was at pre-school. "Go put on some dress pants or something. You look like a soccer mom. Let's go to the police station, ruffle some feathers."

Rivien flipped her sister the bird. "Don't sound so excited about it. I'm counting on these same guys to dig up some evidence in Josh's death too, so let's not ruffle too much."

"Don't worry about it. I'm a fucking ray of sunshine," said her sister as she turned on her high heels, flicked her long hair, and strode up the back staircase to Rivien's apartment.

• • •

At the police station, both Rivien and Edi were pleasantly surprised. Although a duty cop had to respond to the call last night, as it was after hours, the case had already been handed over to the Crimes Against Persons department. The investigator, Inspector Hilts, met them in a conference room, not an interrogation suite. He was older than Rivien, bald, with a muscular physique packed in a short frame.

"It's nice to meet you in person, Dr. Gilrie. Wish it was under better circumstances. I spoke to Dr. Pinder yesterday, and she told us what you had learned about Dr. Landry's death. So that investigation has come to my department too. We are working on warrants to get the hospice records that you mentioned to Dr. Pinder."

"Excellent. I'm glad you guys are on it. I don't really know if there is much else I am going to be able to add to the original request from the ME, but I am going to at least try to round up the testing results from some drugs sent away prior to his death."

"All right," said Hilts. "As long as whatever you turn up goes back to the ME, we can get that information from her. Now on to your case."

Edi opened her mouth to cut in, but Rivien shot her a glance and Inspector Hilts stopped speaking. Things were going smoothly so far, and Rivien wanted to stop her sister from becoming prematurely antagonistic. Edi lived for conflict, and it had gotten her far in life, at least professionally.

"As I was saying," said Hilts, with a sharp glance at Edi, "the officer from last night put in his report that you had been parked out in front of St. Mike's for much of yesterday, and that in your own estimation, this was a likely spot for the needle to have been placed. This morning we went to the facility and retrieved their CCTV footage."

"Already?" Rivien blurted out, tipping her hand to the fact that she really didn't know much about criminal investigation.

"Large organizations like Sacrament have established protocols for such requests, and it is simple to get a warrant for such evidence. And it is always best to try to gather security footage as soon as possible, since some systems overwrite their tapes frequently. We only requested video from the camera facing the street where you indicated you parked. As the street is public property and not even part of the facility grounds, the request clears confidentiality concerns very quickly."

"I'm pleased to hear that, Inspector," stated Edi. *Pleased?* High praise indeed from Edi. *Pleased* was one step away from *impressed*, and Rivien thought her sister might spontaneously combust if someone managed to impress her!

"Yes. I am glad you are here already, Dr. Gilrie. We were going to call you to come in this afternoon. We have your statement from yesterday, but we hope you can make an ID."

"An ID?" gasped Rivien. "So you saw something on the tape? Saw someone doing something to my car?"

Edi placed her hand lightly on her sister's arm. Edi had always instructed Rivien, since the second she got into law school, never to talk to the cops without a lawyer present. It didn't matter if she was a witness or a suspect. Rivien thought it was overkill, but now, even though she was under no suspicion, she felt grateful to have her sister there.

"Please set it up, Inspector," Edi said. "I'd like to speak to my sister privately while you get it arranged." *At least she said "sister" and not "client,"* thought Rivien.

Inspector Hilts seemed to bristle a bit at being instructed in his own job, but unlike the two sisters, he appeared pretty good at swallowing it and moving on. He left without further comment.

"Listen, Rivien. You need to understand that making an ID from CCTV footage is not always easy. And anything you say they can take to court. So if you aren't sure, don't pretend. They will keep looking into it, trying to make an ID another way. Right now, they hope you are the easy way. But if you aren't sure, then you have to refrain from making a guess. Because if anything ends up contradicting that down the line, then any statements you made, about anything, become suspect and you become 'unreliable.' " Edi shuddered a little at the last word, as if being an unreliable witness was an indictment she could not tolerate.

"Understood," Rivien said. "At least it means they saw someone do something to my car. It was intentional, even if it ends up being a fluke that it was my car."

"We're ready." Inspector Hilts's strong voice came from behind, causing them both to turn, Edi coolly and Rivien like a coiled spring. "Come this way, please."

Inspector Hilts gave Rivien instructions in the same vein as Edi's as they walked down the hall, encouraging her to be honest about any ID she might make, and also about her surety. As Edi and Rivien were seated in a small interview room, another officer was inserting a USB drive into a laptop computer with a large screen. Inspector Hilts stood behind the women while the second officer manned a wireless mouse from off to the side of the table. Rivien had an unobstructed view of the screen.

"We'll scroll through the footage a few times, and we can zoom in and try to clarify the images if we can. You can watch it a few times. There is one view that is our best facial shot, and Officer Williams can pause it there for you."

Rivien fell silent as she fixed her eyes on the screen. The black-and-white picture showed the area in front of St. Mike's. Rivien was pretty sure she could see Jesus's feet poking into the top of the frame. *That guy is everywhere!* she thought. *When you are a Jew from the sticks, you really can't escape that man. FOCUS!* Rivien easily recognized her car. Although its bright blue color was not visible on the film, she knew the shape of the car well, although she could not see the license plate.

The officer noted the time stamp and then fast-forwarded, not stopping to highlight any of the many people walking past the car. He obviously knew which part he wanted her to view. Seconds later he slowed the recording as a short, round man in a baseball cap and open jacket approached her car on the sidewalk side. He looked around a few times and paused at her back passenger-side door, although you could not see what he was doing. Edi leaned back, apparently recognizing right away this was not a slam dunk for court. Then the man on the video walked away.

"Wait!" exclaimed Rivien. "I can't see him from this far back, can you zoom in?"

"Yes, of course, we wanted to run it for you once as it happened. We are going to see if we can find other camera angles from any other cameras in the area, but right now we will pause it for you, and zoom in when he is looking over his shoulder."

As the officer reframed the shot, it blurred and then cleared several times as he inched the action forward and the size up. After about six such adjustments, Rivien gasped.

"I know him. I know who it is!"

"You have to be sure," said her sister. "Take your time."

"I am sure. That weaselly little bastard. That's Michael Clubb. The friggin' lackey at the hospital pharmacy." No one else spoke. Now that she knew who was responsible, she was going to wring his neck the next time she saw him. That visualization made her feel better. The thought that came next did not. It unnerved her. She knew who, but she didn't understand why.

CHAPTER 29

The sisters picked up Indian takeout for a late lunch and took it to Rivien's deck. Rivien opened a bottle of dry Gewürztraminer and sat down to strategize.

"I don't get it," Rivien moaned. "Why would he come after me?"

"Was he covering his tracks? Could he have screwed up the meds for that botched MAID you told me about?"

"No, that can't be it. He's a conscientious objector, same church as the hospice, and they don't believe in MAID. So he didn't participate in that." Rivien took a sip. "I have a friend at the hospital pharmacy, and she did wonder if Michael was tampering with returned MAID medications."

"But you said the meds from the botched case didn't get returned."

"Yeah, not those, ones from previous cases. They had been sent off for testing. That was when suspicion was first raised about Dr. Landry, that he might have been diverting meds. Returning watered-down versions and then stockpiling the real leftovers to use on nonconsenting hospice patients."

"And this Michael was involved in that?"

"I have no proof, but my friend told me what she saw, and I put it in the report I'm writing for Karen. The meds that were sent away for testing aren't back yet. They wanted to send the ones from the MAID case the other day too, but like you said, they never got returned."

"Could Michael know you suspected him of the medication tampering? Didn't that happen before you even took on this case? It's only been a few days, right?"

"Yes, those meds were sent away before I heard about any of this. I don't think he would know, and Christina, my friend, definitely wouldn't have told him. But maybe he saw us together, maybe he felt like Christina was suspicious. I don't think she made any secret of the fact she didn't like him. Maybe another staff member told him I had talked with her before I had my blow-up meeting with their boss."

"Him coming after you makes it pretty clear you are onto something—we just don't know what. Maybe he was covering his tracks for trying to get the doctor in trouble, especially now that he is dead. Maybe he feels guilty."

"But then why come after me? Won't make him any less guilty. And he's so incompetent as to be caught the next day? I'm still missing something."

"And you should continue to do so. Let the police handle it. They are doing pretty good so far, and this has to make them more suspicious about Dr. Landry's supposed suicide too, so that is good."

"You're right. This could have all died with Josh if they continued to throw all the blame at him."

"Maybe tomorrow I will drop in at the station, see what I can scare up," Edi said. "See if they will give me any info before I have to head home. You are the victim here, so I'll push them for whatever info they can share."

"I'm going to prep my final report tomorrow. I really don't think there is any more I can give to Karen right now. I have the info from Nurse Pike about the TCAs found in Josh's car. And I will highlight the suspicion about Michael—the med switch thing, anyway. Christina said I can give her name if anyone wants to interview her. I'll give Karen the name of the lab testing the meds and she can light a fire under their ass."

"Do you think any of this will go anywhere?"

"I was hired to look into deaths that may have been associated with Dr. Landry. Priyana was too. But he's dead now, so that line is pretty much dried up. There's more questions now about how he actually died, and if it had anything to do with patient deaths, maybe as motivation. And if there is anything suspicious about Josh's death, then it could open up a whole can of worms. But that is firmly outside of my jurisdiction. I'll let the professionals take it from here."

"Promise?"

"Promise. I will go get Rita in an hour, pick her up a bit early so we can have some fun time."

"I have some work calls to make here. You go get her when you're ready and I'll get my shit done so I can play with her tonight."

"Hope you like make-believing dragons, because that is her whole jam right now. I have dress-up wings and everything."

"I think I can make that happen."

"The logic, or total lack thereof, might get to you after a bit," Rivien said, laughing. "The commitment is strong, the belief sincere and firmly held. The rationality and internal consistency—not so much. Oh, to be a preschooler."

"Hey, I get that every day in court. I think I can cope. And if not, I grabbed my bag of makeup as I walked out the door, so I can distract her with some face painting."

"She'd love that."

The two women sipped their wine and listened to the sounds of the small city. Quiet and calm, not even a distant siren to interrupt the peace. That afternoon and evening, Edi and Rivien both managed to forget the day's events, distracted by more pressing and giggly matters. Even when Rivien stopped to swallow her evening dose of post-exposure prophylaxis, she wasn't holding a grudge or focusing on her bad luck. She was watching her daughter and her sister, flapping their pretend wings as they soared around the apartment.

CHAPTER 30

Rivien was called back to the police station the next morning to give a formal statement about her interactions with the suspect, and to answer some more questions. The two sisters had dropped Edi off at preschool, a much-prolonged affair as Rita demanded to show her "Auntedi" her favorite play stations.

"And this, this is where we play post office. And this, this is the water table…and this, this is my cozy cube."

"Cozy cube?" asked Edi. "What's that?"

"If I'm tired, or I need space, I can go here."

"Need space? You're four, child! Why do you need 'space'?" Edi grinned at her niece.

"Sometimes the other kids are loud. And I like to have quiet time."

"I hear you, kid. I wish I had a cozy cube."

"You could make one in your office!"

"Maybe I can get one like yours."

"You won't fit," Rita said matter-of-factly, before bounding off to chatter with a friend.

"That's me told, I guess," said Edi. "Did your kid just call me fat?"

"No, she said you wouldn't fit in a playhouse made for children. It wasn't a burn."

"I don't know about that. The kid is a wise soul."

"Don't I know it," Rivien said as they left the preschool and headed to her car.

"Let's head to the cop shop together," Edi said. "If everything is good there, I'll head home. I've got court Monday, so I need to prep."

"I'm fine to go on my own, Edi. I don't really want it to look to the cops like I can't fight my own battles," Rivien replied.

"Listen. If they are bringing that suspect in for questioning, I want to be sure the cops understand the possible reasons he has to target you. Then they can take over looking into the background, and you can finish your report and get back to the wine."

Inspector Hilts met them at the station, and once they were seated in a comfortable interview room, Rivien reviewed for him all of what she and Edi had discussed the previous afternoon.

"I don't know if we are going to be able to prove it was Mr. Clubb who tampered with the medications in the hospital pharmacy, or that he targeted you because he felt you were onto him," Hilts said when she was finished.

Rivien opened her mouth to speak but Edi interjected, "Possibly not, but you can still take a statement from Christina, Rivien's contact at the pharmacy. She is willing to answer questions. You should be able to put some pressure on this man. And there's the video evidence too. You do not need to know his motivation to charge him. However, as Rivien has explained, this case intersects with Dr. Landry's death, so there is certainly benefit to you to press this man for information."

"You're right. He can be charged without us understanding his motives. The syringe had a few partial prints too, so that would serve as confirmation if the lab can match them to Mr. Clubb. But I can't discuss the investigation into Dr. Landry's death. We are speaking to the medical examiner, and should we need to interview on that matter, we will contact you in the future."

"That is satisfactory," said Edi. "I would be happy to accompany my client to any future meetings as well."

Holy man, thought Rivien. *She really can be a terror—or terrier—or both.*

"Consider your territory sufficiently marked, Counselor," said Inspector Hilts.

Rivien jumped in, as the cop-lawyer stare-down was getting a bit intense.

"Really, thanks a lot for testing the needle so quickly. I very much appreciate it."

"It was an assault, and we take that very seriously here. I have no problem making sure the suspect understands the weight of the situation, and, as your sister has pointed out, that leverage could be useful."

"But the harm to my sister will remain in the foreground, I presume," Edi said. "Any deals or offers to the suspect will still ensure he is punished for his crime?"

"Whoa, whoa. I don't think I need to tell you that he hasn't been convicted yet. And it's the Crown that decides on charges and pleas, but yeah, I don't think anyone is going to take kindly to assaults on doctors."

"Especially since this is now the second time my sister has been attacked for doing her job," Edi shot back.

"Of course, we have not forgotten."

"Thanks, thanks again," said Rivien. Every time she sort of forgot her past, or at least pushed it away, it sprang back. Edi was right: screw this noise, go back to the wine store, and no more getting pulled back in.

"Anything else you need from us, Inspector?" Edi asked.

"No, and thank you again for your cooperation. I will be in touch if charges are laid, and then victim services will be in touch about court dates and so on. If you are needed to testify, the Crown will reach out."

Edi and Rivien both nodded and shook the Inspector's hand before gathering their coffee cups and exiting the building.

"Wanna grab some brunch before you head out?" Rivien asked.

"You sound like Mom. Always thinking about the next meal." Edi laughed.

"What else are Jewish women supposed to do? Think about eating, talk about eating, and then eating. That's kind of the job description, isn't it?"

"You're not quite a yenta yet, although I can see you're working on it. Anywhere to get good lox in this town?" Edi asked. Rivien knew she was not wowed by the majority of culinary choices in Coulee Butte.

"Do you think that we've got a Jewish deli I've somehow been hiding from you this long?"

"Why don't you open a deli counter in the wine store? These gentiles could use some good Jewish food."

Rivien was about to ask if there was anything else Edi thought she should do with her life, when she stopped short on the front steps of the station.

"What is it?" asked Edi, looking back at her sister rather than at the target of Rivien's dagger stare.

"Fucking rat bastard" came Rivien's reply, stated loudly and not even pretending to be under her breath. The exclamation snapped Edi's head back around until she found the source of her sister's contempt.

"I advise you not to address my client in that manner" came the curt direction from the man standing next to Michael Clubb.

Michael looked dowdy as ever despite clearly wearing his best Sunday suit. He stared at the ground. The man who had spoken was tall and muscular with an impeccable gray suit, a dark blue shirt and tie, and highly polished brown shoes and belt. He had salt-and-pepper hair that was thick with a touch of wave around the ears but cut tight on the neck. Rivien wasn't fooled. She could see the telltale rows of hair plugs and the immobile forehead of heavy-handed Botox treatments. His look screamed *lawyer*, even in this small city. Appearance was this man's currency, and he clearly thought he had money in the bank. Edith and Rivien knew, as would many women, that it was false armor.

"Excuse me?" came Edi's tight retort. Rivien could see her little sister gearing up for a fight, but in the most professional manner possible. Rivien thought watching two lawyers argue was as close as we got in modern times to watching two dandies slap each other in the face with leather gloves. "She was not 'addressing' your client, she was making a comment, and you do not get to dictate what she says."

"We are here to make a statement, not to engage with you."

"Absolutely fine with us," replied Edi. "I assume I can get your card from the inspector, for when we file a civil case against your client."

Michael's head snapped up and his lawyer opened his mouth, before closing it silently. Rivien was a bit taken aback, having never even discussed the possibility of a civil suit with Edi. But she was not one to let her sister have all the fun.

"You little bastard," she said, this time directing her comments squarely at Michael. "What if my daughter had found the needle? I don't know what you think I did to you, but you are going to pay for this. You could have hurt a child, you—twat."

"I'm sorry, I never meant—" Michael stammered, before his lawyer grabbed his arm roughly and whispered, "Shut your mouth." Michael again looked down.

"My client maintains his innocence, and we look forward to seeing you in court, if the police do not drop this ridiculous line of inquiry right now. If you think you have a civil case, then we will see you in court, and I will be happy to take your money." With that, the lawyer led his client up the steps and into the police station, pushing between the women. As they passed, Rivien realized that she had seen the lawyer before, although she couldn't place him. She didn't think he was a former patient. Maybe she had seen him somewhere else in town.

"Looking forward to seeing you both again too," said Edi, with perfectly acidic sweetness, a facade so disingenuous it always hit its mark. You wouldn't want to fuck with Edi.

"Those fuckers are going to rue the day they crossed my sister," Edi said as she strode toward the car. *Yes, yes, they are,* thought Rivien, but she couldn't shake the feeling she was scratching the surface of the men in this situation who deserved her wrath.

CHAPTER 31

After a brief brunch together at a Mexican hole-in-the-wall that served amazing food, Rivien took Edi back to her car.

"You are not going back to that hospice, right?" Edi asked. "You can work on your report and submit it when done?"

"Right," Rivien replied. "I shouldn't need to go back there—ever—not if I can help it. I need to wrap up a few things, but that's it. I will finalize my report, grab a chance to debrief with Priyana, and then I should be back to unpacking wine in the next day or two."

"As it should be. Let me know if Inspector Hilts gets in touch about charges, or if you get a subpoena or anything. If Michael is going to fight the assault charge, I'll connect with the Crown here."

"Thanks, Edi, for everything."

"You bet. Glad I got to see the squirt, even if it was a quick visit. She is changing so fast. You guys need to come up for a visit soon."

"We will. Once I get everything ready here, but before we open, we'll get away, maybe hit the waterslides or something."

"Sounds good. I better get going. I got work to do."

"Love ya, sis."

"You too."

Edi climbed into her sleek SUV and pulled away. Rivien could see her hitting the hands-free phone and talking before she rounded the corner.

Rivien went upstairs and grabbed her laptop, then sat out on the deck to compile her report for Karen. She decided to include the incident at the police station. She felt that since official charges were going to be leveled at Michael, this was not hearsay or gossip, but might be germane to the case. She knew of no other possible motive for Michael's actions, so she thought she should at least mention it.

The Michael situation kept gnawing at her, making it hard to keep the words professional when all she wanted to do was rail against the idiocy of the man. *Supposed to be a man of God, what a joke. Wonder what Gerald would think of this? Does he know that his little lackey is out assaulting women in his spare time?* Rivien also wondered what Nurse Pike would think about all this. She went to the same church as Michael and Gerald, but she actually seemed to have real values. She should know about this, or at least Rivien wanted to be the one to tell her, to see how she responded.

I promised Edi I'd let this go, but this doesn't really count. And who would be concerned about her meeting up with a nun? Not an actual nun, but the next closest thing.

Rivien dug around in her computer bag and fished out her notes. She found Nurse Pike's number, surprised and also grateful it had a *Mobile* notation next to it.

Rivien dialed and was happy to hear the calm and clear "Hello" on the other end.

"Hello, Nurse Pike, I mean Margaret. This is Rivien Gilrie calling. I was wondering if you are free to meet me for coffee this afternoon? I'd really appreciate it."

"I don't drink coffee, dear, but I do enjoy tea. Is there something on your mind? Did something come up with the investigations?"

"Sort of. I want to fill you in, since you've been so helpful to me. And I want to get your take on something."

"I am off work today and I could meet you in about half an hour. Is that suitable?"

"Yes, that's perfect. Want to meet at the Lakehouse Café downtown?"

"Excellent, yes. I will see you there soon."

Rivien pecked away at the report for a bit longer but couldn't shake the feeling she was still scratching the surface. The issue she had been hired to investigate seemed in the rearview, and yet she still felt she didn't completely understand it. This whole mess started with a hospice administrator launching a complaint against a doctor for some unexpected deaths. Actually, it had started with a hospital pharmacist being suspicious of a MAID doctor. Or did it somehow start even before that? Was it about ideological difference and sowing distrust, which allowed half-truths to grow unchecked and fester? *One thing added onto the next, until it couldn't be stopped, and now we are here?*

Rivien grabbed her bag from the deck and moved her computer inside to her kitchen table. She unloaded the dishwasher and then headed downstairs and down the street to meet Nurse Pike.

As she strode into the brightly lit coffee shop, Rivien caught a glimpse of the stately nurse already seated in the back. Rivien got herself a red-eye chai latte and weaved through the tightly packed tables to a more open area in the back. The back wall of the café had large windows that were tilted open to let in the fall breeze. The walls were exposed brick, a testament to the historical nature of the small city's downtown. Coulee Butte was an agricultural hub, positioned near the junction of two major rivers used early in the province's development for transport, and then irrigation. Prior to that, the settlement had boasted a fur-trading post and of course, before that, various Indigenous settlements, including a well-known buffalo jump. The coulees had been a site of much death, but also sustained life and contributed to the survival of the Indigenous people, and all those who came after them.

The walls of the coffee shop currently boasted a display of black-and-white line drawings of heritage homes and buildings throughout town. Rivien found them sterile, but in a resolute way. She wouldn't say they expressed beauty or comfort; they exuded stability. *Lots to be said for stability,* Rivien thought.

"Hello, Margaret. Thank you for meeting me. I really appreciate it."

"My pleasure. Now what can I do for you? You mentioned you wanted my opinion on some matter?"

"Yes," said Rivien, glad for the pleasant but direct nature that was the nurse's calling card. "I wanted you to know about something that happened to me the other day, because I think it happened at the hospice."

"What do you mean?"

"A needle, with a syringe, was pushed up under my car door, and I got poked by it at home, in my garage. I think it was placed there when I was speaking to you the other day."

"Oh my goodness," she said, crossing herself unobtrusively. "How awful. Are you okay? Have you reported it?"

"Yes, I'm fine. The MOH recommended I take HIV prophylaxis for a month, so that is a bummer. And I did report it to the cops. That's really what I wanted to talk to you about. They've brought someone in for questioning, and I believe he is going to be formally charged, but I'm waiting for the confirmation. I think you know him."

"Know him?"

"Michael Clubb. He is a pharmacist at the hospital."

"Yes, I know him. From church. But why would he do such a thing?"

"That is what I was hoping you might be able to help me figure out."

"I most certainly could not hazard a guess about what would make a person do such a wicked thing."

"No, I know that. I don't think you knew, but Michael was apparently the one who initially raised concerns about Dr. Landry to Mr. Strong. Or more correctly, it was Gerald that raised the concerns and then Michael supported them, based on some concerns he had from the pharmacy. Those two were heavily involved in triggering the investigation of Josh, and I'm struggling to understand why that would translate to Michael targeting me."

"It makes no sense. They had raised the concerns, correctly or not, but you were simply doing your job—investigating. Are they sure it was Michael?"

"The cops have video from the hospice."

"Oh dear. I do not like to deal in gossip…"

"This stays between us, of course. I really need a window into their thinking. I can't process it."

"Michael has always wanted to please Gerald. Gerald's position, upholding Catholic values for the health system, places him in high regard within the church. He certainly does not shrink away from the admiration."

"So why doesn't Michael go work for Sacrament, then? Why does he stay in the public system? Sacrament must need pharmacists too."

"Yes. Several years ago Michael did work for Sacrament, but he left after some unpleasantness. He had a bad habit of propositioning younger staff, young nurses. He was married at the time, and his behavior made the women uncomfortable. The manager at the time, before Mr. Strong, let him go. After some time in community pharmacy, he went back to the hospital, but I believe he has been trying to get back into Sacrament's good graces for some time. He has thrown himself into church service, almost as a penance, and it is difficult now to join a church committee without having the, ...pleasure of Mr. Clubb's assistance."

"I get what you are saying," Rivien said.

"I would never say it directly. But yes, I'm sure you do."

"Do you think Michael did this to me, thinking he would gain favor in the church? With Gerald? It seems the opposite of good Christian behavior."

"I am sure it would not surprise you, Dr. Rivien, that deep down, some religious folks are hypocrites."

"I'm sorry, I didn't mean to give that impression, especially about you. I'm—"

"It's okay, dear. I can understand why some people feel that way. I see it too and it shakes even me. But you need to be honest with yourself as well."

"So do you think I'm reading too much into this? Their targeting of Josh, trying to get him in trouble. Am I seeing a witch hunt—an inquisition—where there isn't one?"

"I didn't say that. I would love to believe the motives of my fellow faithful were pure, but I am not sure, not in this situation. Greed, vanity, power. These should have no place in the church, and yet it would be a total fallacy to believe they do not exist, do not exert extreme pressure at times. Michael is not a strong man. And Gerald? I used to believe his faith was pure, even if he was often too concerned with trying to prove it. But there are good people, Rivien, in our church and in our world. I don't want you to lose sight of that."

"You wouldn't be the first person to caution me against painting all people with the same brush. My dad liked that expression."

"Belief can be a powerful motivator, but it doesn't always mean the resultant action is good. But belief is not the only driver. Power, control. Their influence is a cancer. It is what has allowed the board of Sacrament to turn away from our mission. Instead of caring for those who need us, in all ways, they strive instead to exert their control over things they find unpalatable."

"If the cops find out that what happened to Dr. Landry started with spite, and it eventually led to his death, they are going to have to answer for that, aren't they?"

"I don't know, dear. The board, the church even, has been protecting itself, its place in the world, for centuries. They have lawyers, and status, and they will not be easily moved. No one wants to give up power, or position."

"Yes, I met one of the lawyers, the lawyer that Michael had with him at the police station. He and my sister—she's a lawyer too—got into it a little bit."

"He was representing Michael? I would suspect he was from the church then, or at least associated."

"Yeah, he was a really slick-looking guy. I feel like I've seen him around before, but I couldn't place him."

"Was he an attractive man, graying hair?"

"Yes, expensive suit."

Nurse Pike reached for her cell phone in her handbag. After some remarkably quick scrolling, she turned the screen toward Rivien. "Is this him?"

"Hmm. It's too small. Let me see." Rivien took the phone and enlarged the image. "Yeah, I think it is. Wait. I recognize this picture too. Isn't it the picture of the board? You and I looked at it on the wall at the hospice."

"Yes. That is the current board of St. Michael's. This is from their website. That is Mr. Kevin Andrews. He is co-chair of the board."

"It makes sense that he's representing other church people. Even asshol—I mean jerks."

"He really is not part of the church anymore. He was raised in the faith but has been absent from religious life for some time. He still is active on the board, though. I have met him at several fundraisers for the hospice, despite never seeing him at church."

"That's the thing, isn't it? This is the only hospice in town, so even if you don't go in for the religion stuff, if you want people to have a nice place to spend their remaining days, you kind of have no choice but to support the Sacrament machine."

"I am afraid you and I will likely never see eye to eye on the role the church should play in the care of our dying. I do think our role exists, to be a safe place of kindness and respect for human dignity. I feel that too often, especially now, we let our pride get in the way of our mission."

"I can support that. And for what it's worth, any patient would be lucky to have you, and anyone like you, with them to the end. Church interference or not. You are what all church folks should aspire to be."

"I thank you. This whole unfortunate situation has definitely made me question some things. But I cannot separate who I am, what I do, and what I believe. It is all one. But what I can do is try, every day that God is willing, to bring peace to those around me. I feel that, in your own way, that is what you want to do too."

"Yes, I guess. I'm not generally short on conviction, or on telling people what I think they should do. It's just not based on religion."

"But it is belief. Without that, there is no compass. I fear that Michael has never truly known real belief; for him, it is performative only. That will never be a good way, and it has led him so far off track, once again."

"Agreed. And he and Gerald were definitely conspiring. Be careful. They obviously know you are a woman of faith, but you are also a woman of reason. I don't want them to know you were helping me, because I don't want them to see you as an enemy. We still aren't sure what happened with Dr. Landry, but between Josh and the needle in my car door, they don't seem to appreciate resistance."

"You needn't worry about me, dear, but I do appreciate your concern. That is the beauty of faith, which I think you have yet to feel in your life. It is a great comfort. When you have faith, you believe in yourself. The righteous ones take responsibility for being the best they can. The less righteous, they may take belief as a permission, or an excuse to not reflect. I know who I am and what my role is, and I will continue to serve, without much care for outside opinions."

"Honestly, it sounds kind of magical. The certainty."

"It can be freeing in its way. You will find it one day; it needn't be religion to be faith." With that, Nurse Pike squeezed Rivien's hand and then rose like a vision and left the café.

Rivien sat quietly, not having expected to have a discussion on religion and faith, not having planned to be so affected by a woman so different from—but also similar to—herself. Rivien wondered what her life as a doctor would have been like if she had the principles of Nurse Pike. Even in the face of the pain, the manipulation, the difficulties, she felt there would have been peace. She couldn't quite picture it.

CHAPTER 32

Rivien headed back down the street to complete her report. However, as she approached her front door, she looked at the adjoining shop space and her papered-over windows with their Coming Soon sign and felt guilty. Why was she still letting this investigation shambles pull her away from her new venture? Instead of heading up to the apartment, she opened the door of the commercial space and stepped inside to look at her partially filled shelves. She decided to take some time printing up her shelf labels, based on the tasting notes she had compiled from her classes and personal exploration. The report could wait a few hours; she could work on it tonight once Rita was down.

After a few hours of store prep, Rivien felt better about herself and the situation. Her contract gig was almost done, and she was happy in the store, putzing away. She hoped it remained that way when she had customers and expectations. As she was about to head up to the apartment to tidy up before preschool pickup, her cell phone rang. She fished it from her purse on the third ring. It was Edi.

"Hold on. I'm just getting upstairs."

"Yeah, I just got back to the office too. But I've been on the phone, digging, since I left."

"Digging into what?" Rivien asked, kicking off her shoes and heading to the couch.

"That lawyer, the asshole with Michael."

"I actually found out his name."

"How?"

"I ran into a nurse that works at the hospice and told her what happened. I figured it will be public soon anyhow."

"And she knew him?"

"Yeah, he's on the hospice board. What were you digging into? You all ready to launch a suit or what?"

"No, I mean, yes, but that's not it. I can't stand lawyers like him. In five minutes he rubbed me the wrong way. All macho bravado. Anyway, I didn't get a card so I got his name from Inspector Hilts. I was driving anyway so thought I'd make some calls, see what I could find out. I don't really know any lawyers in Coulee."

"So whatcha find out?"

"At first, same as you. He used to be on the board for all of Sacrament Health at the provincial level. But in the last five years, he was co-chair of the local St. Mike's board. I figured he knew Michael because they went to the same church."

"According to the nurse, the lawyer doesn't go to church anymore."

"Hmm. Anyway, he's still connected with St. Mike's. But that doesn't really matter to me. My secretary couldn't find anything else out, so I decided to call the Law Society. Check discipline records and complaint history. That's all public information, you just have to ask."

"Do you do that for every lawyer you are up against?"

"Yeah, basically. Everyone gets a complaint at some point in their career, so it's actually weirder to have none; makes me think they're pushovers. But yeah, I like to know who I'm dealing with."

"Does he have lots of complaints, or none?"

"That's what's interesting. I got lucky, because when I asked the admin to check the name, she kind of blurted out that his name had come across her desk the day before. She realized her mistake once she said it, since nothing was official yet, but she knows me, and I pressed her a little bit. She confirmed that a complaint had been filed on a Mr. Kevin Andrews, and that's why she was so shocked someone was calling to ask about him the next day, even though he had never raised flags before."

"Crazy. What was the complaint about? Was it something to do with Michael's case?"

"No. Like I said, she really shouldn't have been sharing, but once she let the cat of the bag, I got her to give me the info, instead of me trying to dig elsewhere myself. I told her that would make things even worse, especially since it was her who aroused my suspicions."

"So?"

"The complaint came from Sacrament."

"You're kidding. From the hospice?"

"No, from the head of the board of directors of all of Sacrament Health, not just from St. Mike's."

"What was it about? If he was on the board here and they didn't want him, couldn't they not renew his term, vote him out or something? Maybe they only want churchy people and he'd abandoned the faith. That's not really a legal thing, is it?"

"It wasn't that. It was a financial impropriety issue, and in fact, the complaint did mention the RCMP had been called as well. My contact told me that, hoping I would say that is where I got my information."

"Whoa. Was he stealing from the board?"

"After I got off the phone with the Law Society, I got my assistant to dig into the board documents that were registered with the government. He is listed as the treasurer of the board, officially. And the legal counsel for the board is a lawyer from his same firm."

"Is that normal?"

"No. Lawyers on boards often give unofficial legal guidance, but if the board needs real legal counsel, it should be an outside party. It's not unheard of to use a lawyer in the same firm, but it is a bit of a conflict, especially if it is discovered that the board was not operating with sufficient oversight, and a treasurer was mixing roles with that of legal counsel."

"So he's a shady dude. No offense, sis, but lots of lawyers are. To me just makes more sense why he'd rep a little weasel like Michael."

"But that's not the important part."

"What? Get to the friggin' important part, then, I gotta go get Rita in a little bit."

"Listen, I think I did pretty damn good sorting this all out on a few hours' drive."

"Yeah, excellent, remind me to thank your assistant later."

"Shut up. You want to hear it or not?"

"Yes, please," Rivien said sarcastically.

"The important part is where the concern about the improprieties even came from in the first place."

"Was Gerald going around ratting out everyone at St. Mike's who wasn't a believer?"

"Huh? No, nothing to do with him. My assistant—shut up—actually knows one of the legal assistants at the Sacrament head office. Since we knew about the complaint to the Law Society, I got her to call her friend up and find out what prompted the complaint. We don't have all the details, but her friend did share that it all started with a Freedom of Information and Privacy request they got about two weeks ago. She felt she could at least share that with us since the request itself is technically public info."

"But I thought FOIP requests took months to sort out, all sorts of wrangling back and forth on what could be released and what couldn't. How did you guys get results of that so fast?"

"No, no. We didn't get any results. The board is still doing exactly what you said, putting together their response to the formal request. But something they must have come across in that process of compilation put Mr. Andrews in the frame for some financial misdeed. Maybe that is what the FOIP request was trying to prove in the first place."

"I still don't understand why this is the important part."

"I'm getting there. Stop jumping ahead. The important part is who launched the FOIP request; that is also public."

"Okay…"

"It was Dr. Landry."

"What?"

"Yeah, he submitted it about a month ago. It was delivered to the board in the last two weeks, and now they've forwarded at least some concerning information to the Law Society, and the cops."

"Dr. Landry? He did mention, I think, that he made a complaint against Sacrament but he said that went to the minister or something."

"It's not really a complaint. A FOIP request is sent to the government directly, and then they distribute it to the target of the request. A FOIP request is looking for specific information, not complaining. I've got to assume that Dr. Landry was looking for financials, or maybe clarity on the governance structure or legal representation. Either way, what was uncovered pointed at the lawyer."

"Josh told us he had put a letter in the newspaper about Sacrament's policies about MAID, but I didn't realize whatever else he did became this formal, or could have gotten back to the people here already."

"It makes me wonder if they knew he did that, or thought he might have, and the complaint was launched against him to discredit him, or make it look like vindictiveness."

"But it was Gerald, with Michael's help, that put in the College complaint. Would they have known about the FOIP request?"

"They shouldn't have, but Kevin shouldn't have either. But given he used to be on the main Sacrament board, maybe someone tipped him off. Loose lips can sink ships, even today."

"Maybe he got Gerald to help him. He wasn't in the church anymore but he was on the St. Mike's board, and that is what really mattered to Gerald. But if he was stealing from the hospice, then Gerald wouldn't back him on this, wouldn't help him make Josh look bad."

"It might not have been theft. Could be misappropriation. Using money for the public facility for other purposes. Lining church or even personal pockets. I would suspect that being a health-care facility, with a hospice component, and church support, there would be a huge budget, a lot of moving parts, and many sources of funding."

"So somehow Kevin found out about the FOIP thing, and convinced Gerald and Michael to discredit Josh. Maybe Gerald was even in on the financial stuff. Who knows? That is all concerning, I am with you, but we still aren't at the really important part, Edi, the bit that matters—what really happened with Josh. Did the stress push him over the edge, even if none of that really makes sense, or did they think if their plan to disgrace him as a doctor failed, they needed to silence him for good?"

"I don't know, Riv, but it's possible. Things about the apparent suicide still don't make sense. The meds in the car, the missing MAID medications."

"But it was too late. What would killing Josh have accomplished if he'd already launched the complaint, and the RCMP and the Law Society already knew."

"I don't think Kevin, or Gerald, knew that yet. At least they didn't three days ago when Josh died. The complaint had literally just arrived. Maybe they thought that the FOIP wouldn't come up with anything, especially if the person pushing it was…gone."

"Oh my god. We need to call Inspector Hilts," said Rivien, pulling her phone away from her ear to check the time. "Shit, I gotta go get Rita."

"Do it. I will call him right now. I wanted to run it by you first. I have his direct number so hopefully I can get him today. Listen, don't do anything else about this tonight. Let the police handle it. If anyone else tries to reach out to you, call the police. Understood?"

"Of course. I will let Karen know what is going on. And I had better call Priyana."

"Okay. But only them. Don't talk about it with anyone else. And don't put this in the report to Karen; keep it off the record. This is outside of her scope now."

"I'll get the report together and call Karen tomorrow, if you'll let me know once you have briefed Inspector Hilts. I'll try Priyana later tonight once I have Rita. I don't want her going near them again either."

"Good call. I will keep you posted. I seriously don't know how you manage to get yourself into such messes."

"Thanks a lot. Me neither. Shit magnet, I guess. But at least we can point the cops in the right direction, not let them get away with this. Especially if they did anything to Josh."

"Agreed. They can't wriggle out of this. Too many people are onto them now. Go get Rita, and don't think about this now. I'm on it. Just get the sweetie and hug her for Auntie."

"Deal. Love you."

"You too."

Rivien sprang off the couch and started to jog down the stairs. When she reached her car she stopped, took three slow breaths, and then looked under each car door handle. Nothing. She took three more slow breaths and willed herself to let the last two conversations fall aside. She didn't want Rita to be able to read the anger and fear on her face. She didn't deserve it. She just wanted her mom. As Rivien backed out of the garage, she looked in the rearview, and shut her eyes, one second too long while still moving backward. But in that second she let the mystery go and forced herself to go into full "mom mode." All it took was one glance in her mind's eye to see the bubbly chatterbox she was about to scoop up into her arms. The rest could wait. Fuck it. Fuck it indeed.

CHAPTER 33

Rita demanded pancakes. There was some story about pancakes at school that day, the point of which was the astronomical number of unique toppings. It was all Rita could think of. Rivien put the defrosted chicken thighs back in the fridge, and they set about creating pancake monstrosities. At least it was both entertainment and sustenance, in more ways than one.

"Honey, we cannot put ketchup on pancakes."

"Yes, we can."

"Not with the bananas you already have on that one?"

"But I like ketchup."

"I know that, but you won't like it with bananas. Trust me. What about peanut butter? Then you can even have a few chocolate chips with it."

"Yeah! Let's have that."

"Okay, but you have to eat one piece of the sandwich meat too."

"With the peanut butter?" Rita said, confused and looking at her mom like she was the crazy one.

"No, on the side. So this whole meal isn't basically dessert."

"Pancakes are healthy, Mama. My teacher say."

"I am sure they are right."

After dinner Rivien tucked Rita into bed and they read another chapter in her dragon book. Rita was buried under a metric ton of stuffies, and Rivien heard her singing to herself, or maybe to her animal friends, as she turned off the light. Rivien called Priyana but got no answer. Instead of leaving a message, she sent a text, asking her to call back.

After Rivien was sure Rita had fallen asleep, she took her computer out on the deck to finish, once and for all, her report to Karen. She grabbed an open bottle of wine out of the fridge, and a favorite chimneyed glass, purchased on a trip to Europe in another lifetime. As she plunked down on a deck lounger, she noticed that Rita had apparently scribbled with chalk on the back side of her hot tub at some point in the last week or so. *Good grief,* thought Rivien. *When did that happen, I didn't even notice. Hope that comes off.* It made her smile. Rivien was thankful for her store, and was proud of her past life as a doctor and social worker. But what she loved, really loved, was being a mom. She thought for a bit, taking what could not be called a sip, but more like a gulp, of wine. Wine most often made her reflective, but in a smoothly rounded way, no jagged edges.

What if something had happened to Rita with the needle? Why had Rivien even taken the coroner gig, even short term? Why would she ever want to be involved in anything that could possibly harm her daughter in any way? She knew she should "fight the good fight" and she hated the feeling that she was dulling her light to avoid the encroachment of moths, but that shame was trumped by the desire to protect her child, above all else.

Rivien picked up her PEP meds, and as she washed them down with another gulp of wine, a creeping notion crossed her mind. Rita was an only child and would almost certainly re-main one. Rivien had read lots of books about only children and strove hard for balance in her child's life, trying to limit the "adultness" that surrounded her little one. But there was one truth about single children she had never heard spoken about or addressed. A truth that Rivien could feel with absolute certainty in her marrow. If Rita died, so too would Rivien.

She knew there was no world for her if Rita was ever taken from her. She applauded those parents who could soldier on after such a loss, but the majority of those parents, probably by a wide margin, had other children, or were at least planning to. They selflessly tamped down their sorrow to salvage some joy for their other—or future—children. Rivien knew she had no such calling or purpose. She would hate herself for running out on life for her parents and sister, who would be as devastated as her. But that guilt would crumble under the weight of her own emptiness left alone without Rita. Maybe strong women say "You can't be defined by your children, or lack thereof," but you can say a lot of shit until you stand with empty arms. A single tear rolled down Rivien's cheek as her too-vivid imagina-tion pictured Rita dying in an emergency room bed, injured, or in a palliative ward, riddled with cancer. Then she saw herself walking out the hospital doors and immediately into the path of a semi, turning to face it with peace and release. Her phone rang and she jolted. She thought maybe Priyana had finally called her back. It was Justin.

"Hey, sorry, I was miles away there," she said. "How are you?"

"I'm good, I was calling to see how things went at the police station, with your sister. Sorry I couldn't call sooner. I've been on a stakeout. But I got your texts."

"It's okay. I know they have the right guy, but his asshole lawyer seems to think they can make it go away. Edi put him in his place."

"I would expect nothing less," Justin said with a tinge of sarcasm. He'd been on the receiving end of an Edi dressing down at least once in their brief relationship.

"But it's not just that. Edi found out that the lawyer was treasurer on the board at the hospice and is the subject of a Law Society complaint—something financial at the board. He knows Michael and Gerald the hospice manager too. It was actually Josh, the doc that died, that started the complaint and put in a FOIP request."

"Wow, that's one big nest of vipers. So at least one of these guys was a crook, and they went after the doc, and then you, to throw you off the case?"

"I don't know. They definitely seem to have something they were trying to hide, or at least draw attention away from. But the thing is, I feel like I know the lawyer from somewhere else, like I recognize him."

"The lawyer? I suppose you don't run into them as much as I do, but maybe you did something together in town. Some committee? Event?"

"No, I don't think that's it. I saw him in a picture of the board at St. Mike's. But there is something else…" Rivien took another sip, appreciating that Justin could sit in silence with her; there was never pressure to fill every second with chatter. "Fuck!"

"So who is he?" Justin said, clearly already able to differentiate a Rivien "ah-ha" fuck from an "oh damn" fuck.

"I know where I know him from. It was the MAID provision, the one that I went to with Josh. He was there!"

"What? Why would he be there?"

"Because the priest wouldn't attend. So the lawyer came instead. I guess he had left the church, like the patient's family. So he came to be a comfort."

"So the patient was religious but still wanted to have MAID?"

"People have all sort of convictions, until it is inconvenient for them."

"I wouldn't call dying of cancer or whatever inconvenient."

"You know what I mean."

"Yeah, I know. So this lawyer was at the botched death and then was also representing Michael. So even if he left the church, he still obviously has friends or at least business dealings with people who are still involved."

"I guess. I wish I knew if this Mr. Andrews knew that Josh's FOIP request was putting his actions on the board under scrutiny. The Law Society didn't get the complaint until yesterday, I think, but maybe he had a suspicion even while we were at the MAID provision."

"I know you want to know, but you have to let this go. Your sister texted me and told me she was telling you to step back."

"Oh, great, so now she is ratting me out."

"I don't think it's that. She was around for your last attack, I wasn't. Palladium was bad enough. I think she wants you to be safe."

"Fine. The cops are on it now, anyway, and they always get their man." Rivien smirked.

"Is that a crack at me?"

"Maybe a crack at the Mounties in general, but whatever."

Rivien was silent for a moment and then said quietly, "The lawyer was at the MAID provision."

"You just said that's where you recognized him from."

"That was the one where the patient didn't die."

"Did he say anything? Make a threat about legal action? That seems like a lawyer thing to do."

"No. Nothing. He didn't say anything, but…Jesus, what if…?"

"What if what? Damn it, Rivien, I can't read your mind."

"I know, I know. Sorry. We still don't know why the meds didn't work. The preparing pharmacist clammed up, and the cops still haven't found the remaining syringes that Josh took away with him. But what if the lawyer did something to them?"

"Why would he do that? Could he even have done that? Had access?"

Rivien again fell silent as she played the event back in her mind. She heard Justin sigh, but he gave her time.

Josh got final consent from the patient, then went into the other room to prepare the family. Where was the lawyer? He went back in the room with the patient, to talk or pray or whatever. How long was he there? Could it have been three minutes? Was that enough time? Did Josh have the meds with him? No, he had set them by the patient, near the IV, still in their case, but he did not haul the bulky thing into the kitchen with the family. What if the patient saw the lawyer tampering with his drugs? He would say something, wouldn't he?

"Rivien?" Justin prodded gently.

"I think he did it. He could have."

"Wouldn't that take time, diluting meds, or squirting some out, mixing them?"

"Not if he brought dupes with him; then it would be a quick swap. He could have done it behind the patient's back."

"How could he even have done that, and with what motive?"

"Michael, his fucking client, his church buddy. Michael would have seen dozens of MAID syringes. Even if he didn't prepare them himself, he could have printed up new labels. He'd have access to all that equipment at the hospital pharmacy."

"But if the patient was his friend, why would the lawyer do that? Cause him to suffer?"

"He's not a doctor. Maybe he didn't realize how bad it was going to be. Maybe he knew Josh was starting to cause problems for him, suspected something was going on with the hospice financing. Even if all Josh wanted to do was make it public, to raise his point about public money perhaps being misused in funding a Catholic institution, maybe the lawyer knew there were skeletons in his closet, and it would all come out if Josh continued his vendetta."

"But Michael is a pharmacist. He would have to know the patient was going to suffer. And if he was a church guy, maybe even a friend of the patient, why would he ever agree to that? Do you think he was embezzling too?"

"No. I don't think so. He's not that smart. I bet he thought the sacrifice of one patient was worth it to cast MAID in a horrible light, throwing even more suspicion on Josh, and getting him to stop. Ruining his reputation. He wanted to be the most pious guy in the room, so he'd see this as a mission."

"This is a lot, Rivien. I get that you and I both are maybe a little more sensitive to conspiracies, after what happened in Palladium, but seriously? You think three professionals were all conspiring against one doctor?"

"I think Kevin, the lawyer, was probably doing it for his own selfish reasons. And he looped in the other two, somehow convinced them they were doing something righteous. Or maybe Gerald was even in on the money thing. I don't know."

"Did they really think making one MAID case go badly, or putting in complaints about one MAID doc, was going to do anything? It's not like it was going to change the law."

"In this town it would be the same thing, at least for a while. Most docs are happy to keep clear of controversy, so they don't do any MAID work. Singling out one provider, making them and the whole process look corrupt—it has a big impact in a vacuum."

"What are you going to do with this suspicion? Karen is looking into the old deaths and now Josh's, and I guess the botched MAID too, right?"

"Yes, that patient finally passed. And the deaths are all flagged to the ME now."

"So call her up, tell her what you think, even if it doesn't go in your report. This mess has a way wider scope than what you were looking into. You know she is receptive. And then call the cops. Start with the one on your case, but you have to tell them how you think Michael and the lawyer and Gerald may all be involved in these deaths."

"They are going to think I am nuts."

"Not gonna lie, they might. But there is something there, too many coincidences. Or get Edi to call them tomorrow. They could talk to other witnesses at the MAID provision, corroborate that the lawyer was left alone with the drugs."

"They might say, 'The other thing that ties all of this together is that Josh was a terrible doc who was murdering patients and eventually made a mistake that he knew would get him caught, so he took his life.' That explanation works well, and it wouldn't be the first time a story like that was true!"

"Agreed, but—and I say this kindly—you are not a cop. You need to give this to them and they can look into it. Like you said, the drugs from the case are still missing. Where are they? And if you get Edi on them too, she won't let them drop it. At least it might put the suspects on notice that they are in frame, and if you are messed with again, it will confirm the suspicion for the cops."

"You're right. I'll call the cops and Karen and Edi again first thing tomorrow. I'm done investigating for Karen anyway. I'm finishing the report tonight and I'll send it and follow up with a call tomorrow. After that, I am going to the shop. And I am ready for it!"

"I'm working overnight tomorrow on a surveillance detail, but call me the next day or anytime you need me. Agreed?"

"Agreed. I miss you."

"I miss you too."

Rivien hung up and texted Priyana one more time. *I'm still up if you're free.* Then she lifted her bottle, but it was empty.

CHAPTER 34

That night, Rivien couldn't settle. She couldn't tell if it was her new meds giving her bad dreams, or if she had brought it on herself by spending her evening thinking of worst-case scenarios. Even if she had been deeply asleep, she would have woken to the single-tone text, hovering as she always did between sleep and action.

It was from Priyana. *I know it's late, but I found something in the pharmacy records and I need to show you now. I really think you are going to want to see this. It's on the hospital server, so I can't take it out of the facility. I got the access granted tonight and I've been digging all evening.*

Rivien: *Now? I have Rita. Can't it wait till tomorrow?*

Priyana: *No.*

Rivien: *What is it?*

Priyana: *I can't say it in a text. Can you come?*

Rivien: *I already sent Karen my report, and some shit is hitting the fan with this. I was going to call you tomorrow. We need to step back.*

Priyana: *Listen, this is the smoking gun, and it's not what you expect. We can walk away after this; it will be done.*

Rivien: *All right. Give me 30 min, I have to get someone to sit with Rita. I'll message you when I am on the way.*

Priyana: *Good, come up to the 6th floor, I'm working on a computer up there in the conference room. I'll see you soon.*

Rivien couldn't believe that even after leaving medicine, she was somehow still being dragged to the hospital in the middle of the night. She thought she had put those days behind her. Thankfully, her friend Colleen was a night owl; she had performed several midnight babysitting stints for Rivien when she got called in to see a patient. Rivien knew she could call her, and she would come over. Rivien hated abusing this kindness again but was grateful for it nonetheless. As much as she wished she could sleep, she needed to hear what Priyana had learned. It had to be big to warrant the covert nighttime operation.

Colleen cheerfully agreed to come over, her own children grown teenagers who wouldn't need her to be alert first thing in the morning, and arrived soon after the call. Rivien was grateful their town was small enough that you could get almost anywhere in ten minutes. At night, when most of the traffic lights turned to four-way caution flashers, she made the drive to the hospital in under five minutes. Parking was free and plentiful at night. As she used her still-operational ID scan card to buzz herself into the staff doors, she thought about how much she had always preferred the hospital at night. Being called back, although draining, had always given her a sense of slowed time, when events moved with more leisure than during the day. The hospital could be overwhelming at the best of times, hectic and pulsating. At night it felt, if not peaceful, then at least reserved, a calm sea of marinating chaos, waiting to release when the floodgates were opened again in the morning.

Rivien saw only one security guard at the main desk and one nurse having coffee and playing with her phone as she headed to the elevator, using her scan card again to permit access from the elevator to the converted sixth floor. Without patients, it was dark on the floor, but the lights were on motion sensors and clicked on progressively as she headed down the hall. Rivien was thumbing out a thank-you text to Colleen as she arrived at the conference room.

"Hey, this better be good," Rivien said playfully as she opened the door and stepped inside.

"Oh, I think you will find it enlightening" came the distinctly male voice. Rivien halted in her tracks, until she was pushed roughly from behind and the door slammed behind her. Her phone and scan card flew from her hand and clattered on the floor.

When Rivien regained her balance, she turned to see Kevin Andrews, the lawyer, standing with his arms crossed at the back of the room. Michael was standing against the door; presumably he was the one who pushed her. He reached down and picked up her phone and card. Rivien put her hand out for them, but he did not make any move toward her. Over in the corner, seated and leaning forward, was Gerald Strong. Rivien tried to keep all the men in her field of vision while she scanned the room.

"Where the hell is Priyana? What are you doing here?"

"She won't be joining us," said the lawyer.

"What the fuck do you mean? Did you do something to her?"

"Oh, nothing, other than relieve her of her phone. A professional should really not be so careless as to leave their bag unattended with their ancient flip phone not even password protected. And speaking of professional, I guess I had better introduce myself as we have not been formally acquainted."

"I know who you are. You're his dirtbag lawyer. And you were at the MAID provision too. Don't think I haven't figured that out."

"Yes, well," the lawyer said slowly. "Yes. I am Kevin Andrews. And I am the lawyer for lots of people in this town."

"So what? What do you want? I have already told the ME about all of you, and she will tell the cops." Rivien knew that was only a partial truth, as she had not yet shared her suspicions about Kevin and Michael and the MAID medication error. She had been planning on doing that in the phone call to Karen in the morning. She had no idea what they thought they would accomplish by tricking her to come here, but she was growing increasingly scared by the minute. "What the hell do you think you're doing? Are you going to hurt me, in a hospital full of people? Security saw me come in."

"Oh, we know," Gerald said. "But he didn't see us come in. Michael called him away, to open a door he lost the code to. He didn't see Kevin and me come in later when Michael opened the side door for us."

"There are cameras, you morons. You do something to me, you don't think that is the first thing they are going to check?"

A wicked smile crossed Kevin's face. "But you know who comes to the side door all the time, especially at night, when the cafeteria is closed…"

Rivien looked past Kevin now, to a pile of soft-sided food delivery coolers in the corner. "Jesus Christ," said Rivien, as she realized how much planning had gone into this meeting. This level of subterfuge was not employed for a friendly chat. Rivien glanced at the door as Michael moved six inches to the left to fully center himself over her escape route.

"I'll ask you not to take our Lord's name in vain," said Michael quietly.

"Screw you. He's not my Lord."

"We can leave that way too," continued Kevin. "'There was too much food for poor Michael to carry, so we had to help him carry it up."

"No one will vouch for that. And how the fuck is he even still working? How is he not suspended?"

"He has been questioned, but not formally charged yet. Nothing administration can do. And people certainly will believe, because of the food. Michael is now the hero of the fourth floor. The poor overnight pharmacist buying everyone midnight lunch, even inviting the delivery guys to join him for some themselves. The obvious reason why security didn't see us leave again right away."

"You fuckers."

"Sit down," commanded Kevin. Rivien did not move. "I said, sit down."

"This may come as a surprise to you, but I don't answer to you. I'm not some lackey like Michael here. You can kiss my ass."

"Are all modern women like you so vulgar? Thinking they are tough, in charge, when really, they are helpless and don't want to admit it."

"Like I said, people know I am here. I really have no idea what you think you are going to accomplish. Do you think you're going to intimidate me into silence? It's too late. There are real investigators looking into this whole mess already. However you all are involved, they are going to sort it out."

"I guess we will have to see," Kevin said calmly. "But suspicion does not a conviction make. Your sister must have taught you that. I see no evidence to support any of your claims, just two doctors, one murdering patients and the other guilt-ridden about the death of her colleague."

"I will assuage any guilt I might feel by getting justice for Josh, and clearing his name," Rivien shot back. "And helping prove one of you helped kill him. And you may think you're so clever, but don't you think they will find evidence? Gerald over there stole medications from the hospice that didn't even arrive until after Josh left. You're idiots!"

Rivien realized instantly she should not have let any of her info slip. Kevin got red in the face and shot daggers at Gerald, who opened his mouth but, unlike Rivien, knew when to shut it again. She had given away one ace in the hole, and now she needed to drive it home like a stake to the heart. "So nothing you do to me is going to change that. The cops are now dusting for prints, they are investigating Josh's death. You really think they won't find something?"

Kevin took a deep breath, centering himself again after realizing his co-conspirator's blunder. "That may well be. And if that comes up, we will deal with it. It still won't alter our true purpose. To show the evil of physicians playing God, deciding who will die, killing people, God's creations. This abomination must stop."

"Are you kidding me? Is that what you told these two? That you'd what, come back to the church to save souls? You were afraid of being found out. You've been embezzling hospice money, probably keeping it for yourself. How long has it been going on? Maybe you figured out how to do it when you were on the provincial board but knew you could get away with it way easier here. Is that why you left the church—guilt? Or maybe you never believed at all, just needed an easy place where you could manipulate everyone and they wouldn't question you. Josh stumbled on this, even if it was totally by accident, and it was going to come out because he wouldn't stop pushing. That's why you tried to ruin him, and had him killed."

"Is that true?" Gerald asked Kevin.

"Of course not. Don't believe her. We are in the right," Kevin said.

"But you said we were being soldiers for God. It needed to end."

"And it will. It still looks like Josh was murdering patients," Kevin said.

"Looks like?" said Rivien.

"Gerald. You told me you were not afraid to go to jail, that you were more afraid to do nothing and then face God. I helped you to do what needed to be done. You still got what you wanted."

"I am not afraid to face your God either," said Rivien.

"Good," said Kevin. "Because you are about to."

CHAPTER 35

Rivien was silent. The whole room was silent. Kevin stared at her like a jackal, eyes twinkling, teeth bared in a sickening grin. Gerald watched Kevin. Michael looked at the floor.

Rita. It was the thought that broke through Rivien's mounting panic. *Rita.* The drive to see her grow up had saved her before, and Rivien knew it was her only chance now. She had to find out what they were planning, keep them talking, let them think they had surprised and frightened her. She had to dig in, and she had to stall. Her only hope lay in the penchant of small-minded men for taking any opportunity to try to suppress the superior women around them.

"You're pretty quiet, Michael. You all of a sudden lost your taste for hurting women? Didn't stop you planting a needle on my car. Did they send you to do Josh too? That seems like too much responsibility for them to delegate to you."

Michael did not answer, but Kevin glared at him and said, "We probably wouldn't even be here if that idiot hadn't taken it upon himself to try and scare you with the lamest threat ever. He found out you had talked to your friend at the pharmacy, and he thought you were figuring out our involvement. He thought that stupid stunt would scare you off. Not only did it not work, but he got caught in the process. Needless to say, he has some atoning to do."

"Jeez, Michael, seems like they are making you take the blame. After you more than pulled your weight in the pharmacy, tampering with all those meds, hurting those people."

"I didn't hurt anyone," Michael blurted out.

"Shut up," said Gerald.

"I don't believe that Josh ever tampered with any meds," Rivien stated. "I don't believe he was killing people at St. Mike's, so why don't you tell me how you and Kevin did it. Because I am struggling to believe that Michael could have executed any of this himself."

"But I did do it," said Michael. Kevin lifted his hand to silence him but he continued. "But I didn't hurt anyone."

"You mean besides me?" Rivien said sarcastically. She had gotten Michael talking, and even if all the others did was try to silence him, it was distracting them for the moment.

"I only tampered with the meds that had been returned. I just watered them down when my coworker wasn't looking, then drew her attention to it. Then I arranged the Code Brown so I could do it again. But I didn't hurt anyone. Gerald asked me to do it to get Dr. Landry in trouble."

"Shut up, Michael," Kevin said.

"But why?" Rivien asked. "Because you don't believe in MAID? Are you really a bunch of hardcore zealots? Or just greedy bastards."

"You may think us zealots, Ms. Gilrie—" said Gerald.

"That's Dr. Gilrie. It doesn't go away, you prick."

Gerald continued in a flat voice. "You may think us zealots, *Ms.* Gilrie, but just because you liberal snowflakes have no faith, no compass, does not make you right. Our religion, all religion,

has been around many millennia longer than your woke senti-
ments, which are destroying our world. If more people believed
in God, put their faith in a higher power, our society could finally heal. Instead, we give power to politicians, who make laws to
serve the lowest common denominator. There is no drive anymore, no sacrifice."

"I'd say Josh sacrificed an awful lot, wouldn't you?"

"I saved Josh," said Gerald, standing now and moving
around the conference room table, ready to pontificate, claim
his moment in the sun.

"*Saved* him?" said Rivien incredulously. "You killed him!"

"I saved his soul. He needed to be stopped from committing
more sin. He is at peace now."

"Are you kidding me? How the hell did you even get into his
house? Why would he agree to see you?"

"I went over and told him I was sorry, that I knew I was
wrong. I told him that I knew that Michael was the one tampering with meds." Apparently this was news to Michael, whose
mouth dropped open. "He let me in. He was already pretty
drunk—he did half my work for me. I put pills in his drink
whenever he wasn't looking. I had opened the capsules ahead of
time, and sprinkled the powder in."

"There is no way you could lift him into the car. Or drag
him. How did he end up there?"

"When he could barely stand, I told him I would take him
to the police station, so we could report Michael. He could
barely think, so it really wasn't hard. I got him downstairs,
loaded him in the back seat, turned on the car, and left. He was
so out of it by then he didn't even see me put on gloves to put
him in the car. I waited around to be sure he didn't open the
garage door, which he never did, then I called the cops for the
wellness check. I told them I was worried about him, racked
with guilt as he was."

"Guilt. Guilt over the botched MAID? That was your fault. And you must have taken those used MAID medications with you, after you left Josh's house. The cops know they are missing. But you had to cover up that they were tampered with, probably by Kevin with dummies that Michael supplied?"

The men looked at each other but said nothing. Michael slumped. Rivien realized she had been right, and they had not been aware how much she had already figured out.

"So that poor patient is made a martyr, Gerald gets to be a saint, and Kevin gets to keep being a thieving dick. Are you okay with that, Gerald? That Kevin was skimming from your hospice? Taking money from your church? You know they are investigating him? Since he clearly lied to you about why he was helping, are you sure you don't want to say something to him? Or are you all good with what he's done?"

"The only one who will judge is God."

"Bullshit. You judged the hell out of Josh. And the patients. And what about you, Michael? Still sticking with your 'I never hurt nobody' bullshit? I watched that man suffer. You may not have pushed the syringe plunger, but you caused that suffering. You destroyed that family. Don't any of you get all fucking superior with me. I've already told the cops all this." She didn't clarify that it was her cop boyfriend she told, and not the local police. It didn't matter; the suspicion had been communicated and was now proven correct. They couldn't hide.

Kevin spoke again. "If I hadn't had to go bail you out of jail, Michael, had not seen her and her bitch sister, she probably would never have remembered me."

"You were in the picture at St. Michael's," Rivien said. "I remember it now. When all of this comes to light, they will burn that place down. Maybe the whole fucking organization. It will finally be recognized what a backwards, bigoted system it is to impose your beliefs on people and deny them choice. And you, all you self-important 'leaders,' can go right to hell knowing it was your fault it crumbled."

"No, it won't," said Gerald. "Because we are so much bigger than you. Even if I need to take the blame for Dr. Landry, I will. I will confess to taking those meds, and going over to his house, to give him the opportunity to unburden himself to me. I found him there, drunk, ashamed. I'll pretend he confessed to murdering the two patients in the hospice. You won't be around to contradict that. I will tell them I drugged him and put him in the car. I am not afraid of jail. I stopped a murderer."

"No, you didn't."

"To me he is a murderer. I don't care that the government sanctified his provisions; God did not. I did not. He was a murderer who was going to continue killing until he was stopped."

Rivien stood silently. How do you counter blind faith and ingrained doctrine with logic? She thought religion was supposed to be about compassion, and she knew for most people it was. But history had proven time and again that, blinded by their own righteousness, people will do all manner of inhumane things to those they deem unworthy.

"How did you even know what medication to take? You told me before you weren't clinical, couldn't even remember the name propofol."

Gerald looked at Michael.

"Jesus, Michael, do you really think your hands are so clean here? They have implicated you in everything. You will go down as an accessory to murder. Can't you see that whatever they are planning to do to me, it's you they are going to blame? You are the one that works here. Can't you see what they have planned for you?"

"The only one going down, Ms. Gilrie, is you," Kevin said flatly as he took a step toward her.

"Oh, they'll come for you too, you prick. You met my sister. She will find out exactly what you did with the money, how you stole it, where it went. It will all come to light."

"I doubt that, or if it does, it won't be soon enough. I have places I can go. Either way, it will definitely be too late to help you."

Rivien knew her time was drawing thin. "What is your fucking plan, then? Make me write a suicide note? You think you can kill me in the hospital and no one is going to notice?"

"You are distraught," Kevin continued, clearly now relishing torturing the target of his scorn. "You thought your investigation triggered Dr. Landry to take his life. You had seen a poor patient tortured in front of you, saw his family suffer. The trauma—oh, you poor thing—from your last attack, it all came back. I don't really have to go on. Every disgruntled patient you ever had, every righteous person will be glad that you are finally gone. The internet sleuths will fill in the blanks for us; everyone loves a bit of gossip and a juicy story. Maybe they will think you and Dr. Landry were lovers? I really don't care."

"You don't fucking know me. Anyone who does will know that is bullshit. If there is one thing I can do, it's cope."

"Oh, I know you're a heartless bitch, but I am sure someone will believe you were deeply affected. You came to the hospital, got your friend to steal you some fentanyl from the pharmacy. Michael assures me that is what the records will show. That Christina hadn't counted out tonight's vials correctly, and they went missing on her shift. You asked her to get them for you, told her it was something that would help you relax, help you sleep, and to leave them for you in a certain spot in the hospital."

"She would never do that. Even in your pathetic make-believe."

Kevin prattled on, putting on a show like this was a court-house on TV. Rivien let him talk, her mind busy. She had solved many a problem while pretending to listen to the men around her tell her she couldn't. She needed to do it again now.

"Christina felt sorry for you, she wanted to help you get a little sleep. She didn't think you'd hurt yourself. She knew you were comfortable with injections. And don't worry, tonight, if you need help, we'd be glad to assist. We've got a great supply of gloves in this hospital, so no prints. And not to imply you are a weak little woman or anything, but between the three of us, we can most certainly hold you down so you won't hurt or bruise yourself in any way. Make it calm. And we do have your phone, after all. I believe you have face recognition unlock? Michael said he saw you use it on the curb the day Josh sped away. He was watching for your return from the window. Even a dead woman can type out a message to her sister, or her boy-friend, saying goodbye to this cruel world. You came here, the quietest place in the hospital, no one around, no daughter to find you. And you too took the coward's way out."

Rivien knew she had to make a play. She made up the best lie she could think of, counting on a moment of confusion, of them trying to catch up to her doctor brain and sort through the consequences. "I'm allergic to fentanyl, you idiots. Anaphylactic. Christina knows that. She's known me for years. She would never in a million years give me fentanyl to 'relax,' even if she was the most crooked tech in the world."

Michael stared at the other men. He was the only one with medical training, and his superiors were already turning to glare at him, ready to accuse him of once again messing up a key point in their plan.

Michael stammered, "There's no way...I...I couldn't have known..." He moved toward them imploringly, and Rivien bolted. The second she thought she had clearance to beat the pudgy Michael back to the door, she was gone. She jerked the door open and sprinted down the hall as she heard the torches and pitchforks rally behind her.

CHAPTER 36

R ivien ran down the hall toward the exit arrow on the far
wall. She was fit, faster than the men chasing her, and she
thought this time things were going to work out for her. She
turned down another short hallway, but then she saw the scan
box on the back stairwell. After hours, the nonpublic stairwells
were secured for safety reasons, and she had dropped her only
means of escape along with her phone. To access the public
stairs next to the elevator, she would have to turn back in the
direction of the conference room. She was trapped inside this
box of death. *Fuck, I hate the hospital,* she thought for the
ten-thousandth time.

She could hear her pursuers gaining on her, so she grabbed
for the door to her left and slipped it open quietly and rotat-
ed herself inside. She looked around the dark space, lit only by
emergency lighting, and realized where she was. It was the hospital's simulation lab. She had been there before for lifesaving
certifications, but it had been a few years. She checked the door
to see if it locked but of course it didn't, as it was one of several
old hospital rooms they had amalgamated to make the lab.

She ran to the wall, slamming her hand into the Code Blue button that still adorned the wall. She was not hopeful, and she was proved right. The alarm had been disconnected. Probably one too many zealous trainees pushing it in a fake code. The small hospital could not support their code team responding to "boy who cried code" situations. She could hear the three men opening doors down the second hallway, searching for her. It would not take them long to find her.

She ran to the med cart. It was sitting in the corner, with an older-model defibrillator sitting on top, ready for practice and some "Stayin' Alive"–rhythm CPR. She rapidly dug for syringes and pulled open the medication drawer to consider her options. Medicine is not something you forget, not after the sacrifice made to obtain the proficiency, at least enough so you could sleep at night and get over the fear of killing all of your patients. She found what she wanted—paralytic, fast acting. She loaded the syringe and grabbed a needle, grateful more than ever for the rise of high-fidelity simulation, and the theory of using real meds and real techniques in fake situations. Even if the medication was expired, she knew that didn't mean it was ineffectual.

She heard a door about two down from her open and could hear muffled conversation. Her pursuers would know she was trapped, that she couldn't get out. They did not seem in a rush to find her. As she continued to search for proper ammunition, she forced herself to consider what makeshift weapons her captors could have conjured up in the other rooms. She ran across the room and pulled a familiar tray from the shelves. In her last year of practice, she had helped a friend run an education session on maternal cardiac arrest and perimortem C-section. She ripped open the bundle, knowing she would find a preloaded scalpel; if she was lucky, there would be two. Traditional surgical scalpels are packaged separately, as reprocessable handles and disposable blades. In a maternal cardiac arrest C-section, the drive to save the infant, and to try to resuscitate the mother, necessitated the horrifically termed Splash and Slash. Throw Betadine on the area and make the cut, nothing more, nothing less. As there was not time to open and load a scalpel onto a separate handle, the perimortem C-section kit was one of the few places that the scalpel could be found already assembled.

As Rivien's terror, but also her resolve, grew, she took her supplies and searched for a hiding spot. There were few in the sterile environment. Then she saw that, although one gurney in the practice suite was already occupied by a shrouded practice mannequin, the other was not. She climbed on, pulled the sheet over her body, and held her weapons, one in each hand, down at her side. She was ready to slash and splash.

CHAPTER 37

S he heard the door open, saw the light come on.
"Where the fuck is she?" said Gerald, apparently not too
holy to curse when the situation really demanded it.

"She has to be here," Michael whined. "We checked every
other room, and she couldn't get out the pass door, I've got her
scan card. This is the last room."

"What is this place?" asked Kevin. Rivien pictured him staring at the shrouded bodies.

"It's the sim lab," Michael said. "They do training here, run
courses."

"Well, fucking find her. We can kill her here if needed. It's
still private, and it will look like she came here to be alone. Since
we can't use the meds, then we'll hang her or something. Or slit
her wrists."

"That's only in the movies," said Michael quietly.

"Shut up. This is all your fault anyway. So you have to do it.
I don't really care how. Just find her."

Rivien stayed as still as possible, forcing herself to calm her
breath and will her diaphragm into submission, to move only as

much as needed to sustain her consciousness. She questioned her next move. They would find her, they knew she was here. As she heard them moving around, she steeled herself for the inevitable moment when they pulled back her drape. She thought back to a time in her university days, when she took a "Lady Beware" course with a padded attacker. It allowed the participants to practice their newfound self-defense skills. *Nothing like teaching women about defense instead of teaching men about self-control and consent. NOT NOW, Rivien,* she said to herself. *Fucking focus!*

In the course, even during the simulated attacks, Rivien was the only woman who had screamed. No one could believe it. The one thing you are taught to do, expected to do, judged "willing" if you fail to do, was not at all the natural thing to do for the vast majority of women. Silence was never Rivien's strong suit, and she thanked her lucky stars now for the bloodline of strong and ballsy Jewish women before her that instilled in her, through genetics and wonderful nurturing, that we are done taking shit.

CHAPTER 38

R ivien heard the sheet being torn off the dummy next to her. "Shit!" came the shocked exclamation, Rivien couldn't be sure from whom. She tensed all her muscles.

As her face met the light in the moment her shroud was pulled back, she sprang upright at the waist and unleashed the wail of all mothers separated from their children. She slashed with her left hand and the scalpel. She knew she found purchase as she felt the spray of blood on her face. She'd done well if the cut was deep enough to draw arterial flow. She followed the gush with her eyes and listened to the sound of a scream. She saw Gerald leaning forward, grasping at his face as blood poured from him. She jumped to her feet on his side of the gurney, plunged her scalpel under his chin and ripped up, flicking his head back with her force. The blood caused the blade to twist, and Rivien sliced her own palm. The scalpel fell from her hand as another gush of blood from Gerald hit her and the gurney behind her. Gerald slumped to the ground, grasping wildly at his neck as he gurgled. Rivien wanted to savor it. Blood didn't bother her. She wanted to kick him, stomp on his neck, drive the scalpel clean through to his spine. But she couldn't. She heard someone retch behind her and the clattering of a metal bin on the floor.

Michael was slumped against the large metal shelves, which were shifting on their coasters while he grasped for something to right himself. He was as white as the sheet that had concealed Rivien, until its Jackson Pollock splattering of blood. She whipped her head to the left and saw Kevin at the end of the gurney. He lunged at her once and she darted to the head of the bed, thankful for her smaller frame and the ability to wedge herself through the suction tubing and vitals monitors occupying the head space. Kevin lunged again for her from the opposite side of the gurney and Rivien kicked hard near the floor on her side, disengaging the brake. She shoved the gurney hard at Kevin, just as he leaned over to grab her. The combination of his forward center of gravity, coupled with her push and the slippery mess of Gerald's expanding blood pool, made Kevin slip and fall hard to his side along the edge of the gurney, next to his rapidly expiring co-conspirator.

Rivien saw her chance. She vaulted the gurney, not even trying to land on her feet, and slid to the ground on her knees to one side of Kevin. As he pushed himself up on one arm, Rivien launched herself onto his back, forcing him back down to the ground, aided by the bloody mess and his apparent lack of acknowledgment that this woman could kick his ass.

"You bitch" was all he said.

"You bet" was her counter. With her right hand she drove the uncapped, large-bore needle into his neck and slammed her other hand down on the plunger. She didn't know, or really care, what she hit. Could be artery, could be vein, muscle, hell, maybe even trachea. The paralytic would find its way.

He bucked, twice, trying to shake her. She tried to grab his hair but he rolled and she was thrown to the floor. She went to stand but tripped over Gerald's lifeless body and stumbled face down as she splayed into the blood. She rolled to her back and kicked her legs out in time to make contact with Kevin's groin as he came toward her. He crumpled, but remained standing. She crab-walked backward until she hit the wall and could push herself up against it. She knew the paralytic was not instantaneous, especially if she had hit muscle. Adrenaline made it impossible for her to quantify the force she had applied to empty the syringe.

"I'm going to kill you," Kevin spat as he straightened. Rivien grabbed a metal bedpan from a shelf, the best shield she could find.

"Not only are you not going to kill me—you are going to die. You are dying."

"What the hellll…dyu…put…me…" was Kevin's reply. The drug was working. She was winning.

"It's a paralytic. It's already working. In a few more seconds, you are going to be unable to stand, and then unable to breathe. So you need to decide."

Kevin went to his knees.

"I can save you, I can breathe for you, they have the equipment here. Or I can let you die."

Kevin flopped forward face down.

"Help him. Save him" came a small voice from the corner. Michael was huddled away, occupying the least space he ever had in his life.

"Fuck you," Rivien spat. She could hear Kevin's breathing growing very faint.

"Please, I'll do whatever you want. Don't let him die too. Do something."

"Which of you has my phone? Get it. Now!" Rivien barked. She saw Michael's hand go to his pocket, then the photo of her daughter light up on the lock screen. "Bring it here," Rivien ordered, unwilling to look away from Kevin, and unable to control the phone. "Unlock it, with my face. Now open the call history."

"I don't know how to—" Michael protested.

"It's the fucking phone icon. Do it or your friend dies. He only has a minute." Rivien stood, refusing to shift her focus to the phone; Kevin wasn't dead yet.

"Got it. Help him."

"Dial Justin. He'll be in the history," Rivien commanded. Her Hippocratic oath dragged her, internally kicking and screaming, to the crash cart and the airway supplies contained within. "Put it on speaker," she ordered.

She found gauze to quickly wrap her hand, then retrieved a laryngeal airway device and a bagging unit with enough tubing to reach the wall oxygen, Rivien heard Justin's voice. She ignored Michael's continued pleading in the background.

"Rivien? Is that you? What the hell is going on?"

"It's me. I'm okay."

"What the fuck is happening? Where are you?"

"It's a long story. I'll tell you later. But I have to help someone now, and I'm only going to do it if this loser tells you every-thing—*everything*—that has been going on. Record it please," Rivien asked, as she dropped to the floor and rolled Kevin onto his back, the syringe having fallen from his neck.

"Jesus Christ," Michael said, witnessing his friend's dusky color and limp body.

"He can't fucking help you now," Rivien said as she stared at Michael. "Talk." She leaned over Kevin, checked for the still-present pulse, and then deftly inserted the airway and began bagging. She knew Kevin would be able to recall all these events. He was not provided an anesthetic, just paralyzed while aware. She said she would save him, and she would. She felt no respons-ibility to make it comfortable.

She listened to Michael's sobbing retelling of the sordid tale. She intermittently confirmed to Justin her presence and safe-ty. Rivien interrupted once to demand Michael's unlocked cell, from which she called the hospital switchboard and requested security, who seemed to take no convincing to call 911 and attend her hospital location despite Rivien's unwillingness to get into the details of the chaos. She knew she sounded crazy, but the guard seemed unperturbed despite Michael's yammering in the background.

Then the guard said, "We had a call about you. From another lady. She said her phone had been stolen, and she demanded we check if your pass had been used. It didn't make any sense, but we were trying to figure out how to do that when you called."

Thank you, Priyana, Rivien thought. She wasn't going to be left alone. As she glanced at the rhythmic rise and fall of Kevin's chest, driven not by his weak and cold spirit, but rather by her own skill and fortitude, she was grateful again despite the madness. She was fierce, she was vindicated, and she was alive.

CHAPTER 39

The hospital security guard nearly collapsed as he opened the door to the simulation lab. Blood was splattered all over the floor and walls, and Rivien was busy ventilating Kevin while Michael cowered in the corner.

"What the hell happened here?" gasped the guard.

"Listen, no offense, but I'll wait until the cops get here. I'll tell the story once. But this man, he's going to wake up soon, and he tried to kill me. Do you have zip ties or anything we can bind his hands and feet with?"

"Did he kill that guy?" asked the guard, pointing to Gerald's lifeless body.

"No. That was me" was all Rivien offered.

"What? I…" stammered the guard.

"Listen, I will explain everything when the cops get here, but I am not fighting this asshole again, so please tie him up. He's starting to breathe on his own, so he'll be strong again soon. And keep an eye on that one over there too. I don't think he's stupid enough to try anything now, but you never know."

As the guard moved to secure Kevin, who was starting to

moan and wriggle, Rivien walked over to Michael and yanked the phone from his hand, pulled by Justin's calls of "Rivien! Rivien!" emanating from it.

"I'm here. I'm here."

"What the fuck is going on? Are you hurt?"

"I'm okay. I didn't hear everything Michael was telling you. Did he confess, tell you what they all did?"

"Yes, but some of it made no sense. He was all over the place. But I recorded it, so I have it. Are the cops there? Are you safe?"

"Security is here, cops are on the way. I'll call Edi, see if she can get on a conference call with me when I give a statement. I killed a guy. Another one. Fuck me."

"Oh, Rivien, I'm so sorry. But it was self-defense. That guy told me they were going to kill you, make it look like suicide. Like they did to the other doc. I wish I was there."

"Yes. I know. I'll be okay."

"I'll get a flight out there. I should be there tomorrow."

"Thanks. I'll call you once I'm home. And showered. But now I need to get Edi on the phone. I hear the cops coming down the hall, I gotta go."

"I love you."

"I love you too." It was the first time she had said that to Justin.

Rivien hung up the phone so she could face the cops and put her hands up.

CHAPTER 40

Once the police arrived, Rivien was moved across the hall, with Michael placed in an adjoining room, both being guarded by a single hospital security guard stationed in the hall. An EMS team that was in the emergency room delivering a patient had been called to collect Kevin from the floor and take him to the ED for assessment. He was accompanied by another officer, although he remained silent despite being now able to speak. Gerald's dead body had been left in situ. It wasn't exposed to the public, so there was no need to cover it. Crime scene tape now blocked off the entire hallway. As more and more police arrived to secure and process the crime scene, an officer arrived in Rivien's room to take her statement.

"Listen, I don't mean to be rude, but can you call Inspector Hilts?"

"The inspector isn't on tonight. You have to talk to us," announced the youngish cop, bravado not yet matched by experience and even less so by self-awareness.

"Again, no offense, but I don't have to talk to anyone, and I won't talk until I consult my lawyer, but I really would like to talk to Inspector Hilts. He knows what is going on with this mess. I can't start from the start."

"I don't need the start. I need to know what happened here, why we have one dead body and an injured one in the ED?"

"Again, I would like to call my lawyer and speak to Inspector Hilts, and I really want a shower. I'm not sitting here in all this blood all night," Rivien said, looking at her soaked pants, feeling the tug on her splattered face as the blood started to dry.

"I can't let you do that. The other guy hasn't stopped talking, so you really should want to get your side on record."

"Listen, my friend. I'm not worried about my side. I know the truth, so does Michael. So don't try to play me, please, I'm not in the mood. What I care about is doing this right once, and then forgetting this ever happened. So call Inspector Hilts now or give me my phone and I'll do it. I promise you, he will want to know about this now, tonight, before somebody else fucks it up. You either arrest me, or give me my phone back so I can call him and my lawyer myself. Got it?"

The officer looked her over, and apparently the "I just killed a guy" vibes were coming off strong because he disappeared. About fifteen minutes later, Inspector Hilts came through the door, casually dressed in crumpled pants and a golf shirt.

"Holy shit" was all he said when he saw her.

"Yeah. That's about the shape of it."

"Rivien, I'm very sorry this happened, but we need to get a statement as soon as we can."

"I know. But listen. The first thing I am doing is calling my sitter. She is with Rita and I need to call her now. Tell her what happened and make sure she can stay the night. Second, I am not sitting here in his blood. So find a female officer, and I will change out of these clothes. She can take them, and you can take pictures, and then I am having a shower."

"Let's go to the station, and then we can get that going."

"No, I am not leaving the hospital like this. I can shower in the staff room and change into scrubs."

"I need to—"

"Am I under arrest?" She glared at Inspector Hilts, who gently shook his head. "Then I am going to the staff room in five minutes. If you want my clothes or anything else, get it in place."

"Hold on, I'll find a female officer. We'll take the clothes. Then to the station, right?"

"Yes. I will call Edi once I am changed."

"I'll find the officer to escort you. When you're done she will bring you back here, and I can take you to the station."

"Sounds good." *Sounds good? What the hell was she thinking. None of this sounds good. Fuck.*

CHAPTER 41

Rivien felt protected by her well-worn armor of scrubs borrowed from the staff room, the uniform of her old life comforting in this time of madness. She sat stoically with a cup of bad coffee while she waited for Edi to dial in to the interrogation room. She had reached her sister by phone from the back seat of Inspector Hilts's police car. Justin had called Edi already, before Rivien was able to call herself, so Edi was already in the car and on her way down to Coulee Butte. When Rivien called, Edi was able to maintain her composure and communicate her direction to not say anything until Edi had been patched in to the interview as her solicitor. Rivien had also called her sitter Colleen, but she did not have the strength to tell her what had happened. She didn't want any of it passed on to Rita, even unconsciously. She did explain there was an urgent situation and she would not be home for a few more hours. Her friend assured her she was happy to sleep on the couch, in case Rita awoke and went looking for her mama.

At the station, Rivien started replaying the events of the night, starting with the texts sent from Priyana's phone.

"Oh my gosh. Priyana! They got her phone somehow. Is she okay?" asked Rivien, forgetting that it was Priyana who had alerted hospital security to look for her.

"Yes, another officer is speaking with her. She came to the hospital, so she gave a statement too. She was very worried about you."

Rivien continued her statement, explaining in great detail what happened in the conference room, the various exchanges and the chase that culminated in the bloodbath. The account was peppered with Edi's distant objections and directions to Rivien, and also to Inspector Hilts. When Rivien gave her account of the point where hospital security was called, Edi interjected again.

"Inspector, there is a recording of Michael Clubb describing what happened at the hospital, and also what happened with Dr. Landry. It is in the possession of Corporal Justin Glasgow, RCMP member."

"How did you know about that? I totally forgot, I mean, I don't know what I mean," Rivien said, utterly exhausted and near tears as her anxiety to go home reached a fever pitch.

"A recording?" asked Inspector Hilts.

"Yes, despite the chaos, my brilliant sister had Michael call her boyfriend on her cell and relay the information while she was resuscitating Mr. Andrews. I spoke to Corporal Glasgow before you allowed my client to contact me. The call was recorded, and he will vouch for continuity."

"You know that could be considered a coerced statement, Counselor."

"Listen, you consider it however you want. If anything—and I mean anything—from this whole debacle blows back on my client, I will ensure that the recording is aired publicly, as it is our property and Mr. Clubb knew he was being recorded. I will also ensure the public understands that two of the three assailants were actually under police jurisdiction within the previous forty-eight hours and yet somehow were able to launch this attack. I hope you will not need the recording for evidence, but you should at least bother to listen to it. Maybe you can learn something."

"Thank you for your concern" came the cool reply.

"Listen, I'm not really interested in a pissing match right now," Rivien said. "Can I go home? I've told you what I know, and you can listen to the recording. I'm—I'm done."

"I will be in touch if we need additional information, victim services will be in touch too, and I am sure the Crown will let you know when you are needed for court."

"*If* she is needed for court. If these idiots think they are pleading not guilty, I will do everything in my power to make sure the prosecutor buries them. If they have any sense, they will plead guilty."

"Agreed on that point," said the inspector. "Rivien, come with me and I'll get an officer to take you home."

As Rivien was being taken to meet an officer, she noticed Priyana through the glass in the front reception area. She had seen Rivien and was running toward the glass, waving her arms, following her movements.

"Wait, can I go with her?" Rivien asked.

"Sure," the officer said. "Here, I'll let you out."

As Rivien passed through the locked door and back into the public side of the station, she quickened her step as Priyana ran up to meet her. As Rivien went to speak, she faltered, buckling an inch, but was caught by the tiny woman with the large spirit.

"Come on, come on, child, let me take you home."

Rivien couldn't answer. Instead she sobbed, the release sudden and extreme. She cried and she cried, allowing herself to be buttressed by her little crutch, propped up by the glow of support, of compassion, and of strength. It seeped into her, little by little, until she was able to walk, to be led away, her soul reinflating, her body straightening, her head held high as she entered the night.

CHAPTER 42

Priyana insisted on staying at Rivien's, at least until Edi arrived. Rivien initially collapsed in her own bed, but could not settle and lay awake for a few hours, replaying everything that had happened in the last week. She heard her sister arrive and speak to Priyana, and then Priyana's car pulling away. She did not want to get up, and allowed her presumed slumber to be an excuse to continue her silent reflection. Finally, she couldn't take it any longer, and she got up and moved quietly so as not to wake a sleeping Edi on the couch. She went into Rita's room, where she could hear her daughter's rhythmic breathing, punctuated with occasional words and sighs. Rita had always been a sleep talker, and this early morning, Rivien needed to hear it. She was about to climb into bed with Rita, as she sometimes did, when she decided against it, not wanting to risk waking her daughter. Instead, she took an extra blanket and pillow from the bed, and lay down on the fluffy rug that Rita had fallen in love with on a recent shopping trip. As she was about to doze off, she heard a mumbled "Love you, Mama." Rivien didn't know if Rita was awake or asleep, or somewhere in between. It didn't matter.

She somehow knew it was what her mama needed, in that moment and for the rest of their lives.

"I love you too, baby," Rivien whispered. Then she slept.

● ● ●

"Mama, what you doing down there?" asked a tiny voice. Rivien opened her eyes to see a bright smile and a mess of wavy dark hair hanging down above her. "I almost step on you."

"It's okay, Nugget. Mama wanted to sleep with you but not wake you up."

Rita dropped down hard on Rivien from above. Rivien grunted and Rita yelled, "Bladder buster!" which sent Edi running into the room.

"Oh my gosh, are you okay?" Edi said, looking squarely at Rivien.

"I fine, Auntie Edi. What are you doing here?"

"I came to see you and your mama. Baba is on the way too."

"Yeah! Baba!" Rita yelled, hopping off her mom, racing to the door, stopping short, turning around to grab a favorite dragon stuffie on the bed, and then racing out the door. "Baba? Baba?"

"She's not here yet, honey," Rivien said, heaving herself off the floor with Edi's help. "Wanna have some cartoons till she gets here?" she asked Rita.

"Yeah…yes!" Rita made a beeline to the couch and then pointed herself squarely at the TV. Rivien put on her current favorite obsession and then followed her nose to coffee that Edi was already brewing.

"Thanks for calling Mom last night. I didn't have it in me after the police station."

"Don't blame you. Once I talked her off a ledge and reminded her she can't drive at night, I convinced her to come this morning. She should be here soon."

"Wanna put money on what she did last night after you called her?"

"No. Because I know. If she doesn't show up here with at least three meals, then I'll owe you."

"Yeah, I'm guessing, middle of the night she decided to make buns, and she'll come with three ice cream pails full of frozen soup or chili. Actually, I really hope she does. I could use some of her soup."

"I am not going to say I told you so, and I am not going to be mad that we are here again."

"I don't believe you."

"But on one condition only. I told Mom about this deal too, to save you having to get it from her too."

"What's the condition?"

"This is the last time, Rivien. Seriously. I don't really know why you are such a schlemiel, as our baba would have said, but you are. So this is it. No more cases, no more contracts, no more slipping back into the old life. You run the store, love on Rita, and grow old. Got it?"

"I got it. And I'm not going to argue. I don't ever want to do this again."

"I'm hungry!" Rita yelled from the couch.

"Oh, shoot. What do you feel like?"

"Cereal!"

"Okay, but go potty while I get it. You can have it in front of the TV."

"I'll get it," Edi said. "You sit, drink your coffee. Then go get some more sleep. I got this, and Mom will be here soon."

"I'm not sure I can sleep."

"There is nothing you can't do if you put your mind to it," Edi said, mimicking one of their dad's favorite sayings.

Rivien stuck her tongue out at her sister. Rita happened to catch it out of the corner of her eye. She laughed and said, "Ha ha, Mama!" and then proceeded to do it herself to her aunt, her mom, and then the cat, who was not amused.

"Rita, you watch your shows and play with your aunt. Mama is going to get a bit more sleep, okay?"

No answer, as Rita had turned her attention back to her show, laser focused, but only on the TV.

"Go!" Edi instructed.

Rivien took her coffee with her to her bedroom, but it quickly grew cold on her nightstand as she succumbed to sleep.

CHAPTER 43

Later that day, after Rivien woke up from a very long sleep, she emerged onto the deck and into the early afternoon glow of a beautiful day. Rita was coloring on a rolled-out piece of butcher paper while Baba stood guard.

"Come here," Marcia said, wrapping Rivien in a hug, holding back tears.

"Mom," Rivien said quietly, "I don't want Rita to know what's going on, so…"

"So what? So keep it together? Not sure if you think I am getting used to this now, but guess what? Almost losing your child does not get easier with time, or repetition."

Rivien looked at her, and then hugged her again.

"I know. I am sorry. I'm glad you're here. Rita needs her baba."

"She needs her mama too. Your sister already told me to not make a big deal of this—but never again, right?"

"Never again. I love you."

"Go see your posse over there. Rita and I have playing to do."

"I'm drawing a dragon world, Mama. See, this is the bridge."

"That's awesome, baby."

"Not a baby!" Rita said, not even looking up from her work. Rivien did look up, to see what her mom had meant, and saw Edi, Priyana, and Justin sitting on the patio furniture under the awning on the deck.

"Hey! How did you get here so fast?" Rivien made her way over to Justin, who rose, embraced her, and kissed her forehead as she held him.

"Here, sit," he said, directing her to a comfy chair, and holding her hand as he sat next to her. "After we talked last night, I went straight to the airport. I booked a ticket as I was sitting there. Managed to get a last-minute flight out and a good connection. A buddy drove me out here from the city."

"I am so glad to see you. And you too, of course, Priyana. Thanks for coming for me last night. You've all met now, I assume."

"Oh yes, your sister and I are old friends now. You are very alike," Priyana said.

"Really?" the two sisters said in unison. They had never seen it, but the rest of the world always seemed to.

"Want a glass of wine?" Edi asked, pulling a white from a chiller that was plugged into the wall.

"What kind of question is that? Yes. I want some wine. I want all the wine," Rivien said.

"We also have soup," Marcia called out.

"Yeah, you really should eat something," said Edi. Rivien tried to stop herself from laughing at Edi turning into their mother, not that she would ever admit it.

"What?" said Edi, confused, not seeing how easily she had slipped into Baba mode.

"It's all good. Yeah, I'd love some soup, Mom, thanks!"

"I'm not even going to ask how you're doing," said Justin. "I'm just going to say this: I am not leaving this house, and neither are you, for three days. We're going to eat, drink, snuggle on the couch, and watch movies." He tried to smile, but she saw a tear in his eye.

"Good call," said Priyana. "The outside world doesn't deserve you, at least not right now."

"That sounds pretty much perfect," Rivien said.

"I am here to run interference with the cops, Mom is on kiddo duty, and Priyana got in touch with Dr. Pinder this morning," Edi said.

Priyana continued. "Karen told me you can call her when you want, but it will be to chat. She assured me your job for her is complete. She got your report, and I filled in the blanks, and Justin shared Michael's recording with her. She will liaise with the cops about the other cases, about Josh. She doesn't want you to worry about them anymore. She's upset, and I think she feels like she put you in harm's way."

"It's not her fault," said Rivien. "As Edi said, I'm just a schlemiel."

"Schlemiel? What does this word mean?" asked Priyana.

"Yiddish for 'shit magnet,' basically," said Rivien.

"Maybe you're actually more of a vigilante?" smirked Edi, but good-naturedly.

"Screw you. I don't go looking for them, scumbags just seem to find me."

"Maybe you should be a cop?" offered Justin. "Third career? Or is it fourth?"

"Forget that! No friggin' way," replied Rivien.

"Come work for the College," Priyana said, getting in on the good-natured ribbing.

"Also—but to you more respectfully than these idiots—no."

Rita burst through the patio door yelling "SOUP!" before she piled onto Rivien's lap, while Baba trailed her with a tray of soup and homemade buns. *I knew it,* thought Rivien. She caught Edi's eye and winked. They knew their mom so well.

"Yum," Rita exclaimed, grabbing a bun off the tray while Marcia tried to keep it upright. Rita ripped off a huge chunk and stuffed the tasty morsel into her mouth.

"Oh my goodness, child," said Marcia, as she fetched Rita's water. "Have a drink."

"This time," Rivien said, "I am going to do what Justin said. Open some good Blanc de Noir, the real good stuff. Watch some Keanu movies and forget the world. Then I am going to go back to selling wine, and minding my own business."

"Yeah, we'll see how long that lasts," said Justin. Edi and Marcia both glared at him.

"This time I mean it. Maybe the jerks will stay out of my way now. I'm getting a rep. 'Not to be effed with.' I plan to capitalize on that. I think I've earned it."

Rivien topped up her glass of white until it touched the rim and she had to lean over to slurp it. Classy as always. Surrounded by love and bright things in the world. Where she belonged.

ABOUT THE AUTHOR

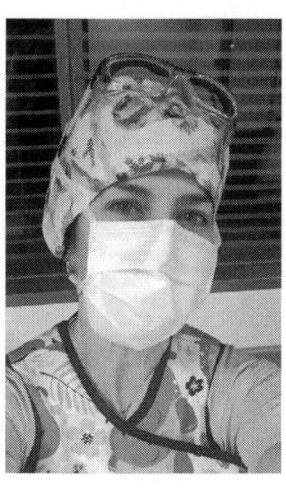

Maren Cliff is a fiction author and a physician from Alberta, Canada. She lives with her partner, young daughter, and a belligerent cat. A self-assessed rolling stone and jack-of-all-trades, master of none; her writing comes from an ingrained need for challenge. When she is not wrist deep in bodily fluids, she enjoys travel, camping, wine, and wine.

MAREN CLIFF

Manufactured by Amazon.ca
Bolton, ON

45400748R00141